The Red Scooty

A TALE OF ROADS, DESTINY AND THE CLOSURE.

Harsh Kumar Arya

BLUEROSE PUBLISHERS
India | U.K.

Copyright © Harsh Kumar Arya 2024

All rights reserved by author. No part of this publication may be reproduced, stored in a retrieval system or transmitted in any form or by any means, electronic, mechanical, photocopying, recording or otherwise, without the prior permission of the author. Although every precaution has been taken to verify the accuracy of the information contained herein, the publisher assumes no responsibility for any errors or omissions. No liability is assumed for damages that may result from the use of information contained within.

BlueRose Publishers takes no responsibility for any damages, losses, or liabilities that may arise from the use or misuse of the information, products, or services provided in this publication.

For permissions requests or inquiries regarding this publication, please contact:

BLUEROSE PUBLISHERS
www.BlueRoseONE.com
info@bluerosepublishers.com
+91 8882 898 898
+4407342408967

ISBN: 978-93-6452-842-9

Cover design: Shivam
Typesetting: Namrata Saini

First Edition: October 2024

Prologue

Did you find your closure?

Jay did, finally.

It doesn't matter from where you're seeking knowledge. What truly matters is your capability to apply it to your life, regardless of anything else.

Preaching can seem effortless, even the easiest task, until you find yourself in the position of applying the knowledge you have been preaching. While it's often said that silence is the most appropriate response, can you honestly find the strength within yourself to choose silence when you're overwhelmed by rage and intense emotions?

That's something you need to develop. You have to train yourself for how you would handle such an amount of stress, agony, anger, and rage.

For this book, I would like to express my gratitude to my wife, my inner strength and to my father, my rock and foundation. She is an extraordinary woman who, despite my decision to put my passion for writing on hold, to focus on earning a living after our marriage, has always encouraged and supported me. It is my father's sole desire to witness my settlement, and I am fully committed to granting him this tranquility.

I was on the verge of burying the draft of this book, but her compliment gave me the motivation to keep going.

'You were more alive before our marriage. What's the reason behind being so lost in your thoughts? Why not write them down like you used to?'

My eyes met hers as I looked at her, trying to decipher her emotions.

'Do you really want me to? It could result in me becoming a different version of myself. Perhaps I won't be able to allocate sufficient time to you in that case.'

'But you would be with me wholeheartedly when you brain fog dissipates.'

That's what brave women do. They let their husband struggle while providing moral support. She revived me.

I have dedicated my evenings to crafting this book, ensuring that readers are captivated and entertained. Ultimately, this book is a creation of fiction. The creation of this book involved the use of ginger-flavored tea and my dedicated laptop, which put in a lot of effort alongside me.

Let's Begin!

Contents

Chapter-1: An Enchanting Evening — 1

Chapter-2: Lord Shiva — 13

Chapter-3: The Wanderers — 27

Chapter-4: Lost and Found — 39

Chapter-5: Escaping the Reality — 53

Chapter-6: Beyond the Boundaries — 72

Chapter-7: Suffer by Choice — 86

Chapter-8: The Pandemic — 106

Chapter-9: God's Plan — 120

Chapter-10: A New Reality — 132

Chapter-11: A Widow's Wail — 145

Chapter-12: The Devil — 159

Chapter-13: The Beginning of the End — 167

Chapter-14: Thing or A Fling? — 177

Chapter-15: A Million Things — 185

Chapter-16: Generation Gap — 193

Chapter-17: The Goodbye — 201

Chapter-18: The Numb Heart — 210

Chapter-19: Social Acceptance — 223

Chapter-20: The Time's Demand	233
Chapter-21: A New Beginning?	247
Chapter-22: The Deadlock	256
Chapter-23: One Last Journey	270
Chapter-24: The Closure	278

Chapter-1

An Enchanting Evening

The Faatak, Jwalapur Railway crossing, which links the main Jwalapur Bazaar to Arya Nagar Chowk, was bustling with people. What drew me here was the mouthwatering sweet samosa. Whenever people had to stop because of the railway crossing, this shop would quickly become crowded. And so, I found myself among the crowd. I parked my bike to make the most of the waiting time.

'Uncle, excuse me, please.' I heard a high-pitched, feminine voice that sounded thin, and it poured into my ears.

A teenage girl, almost seventeen, was making her way to the shop. I gazed upon her face. There was a northeastern influence in her overall look. Small, slanted eyes and a broad forehead. A blanched face with flawless skin.

'I'm not your uncle. Say something touchy and sweet.' I tried to pick on her.

She stared at me for a couple of seconds. I felt a sense of disaster as she stared at me with those chubby eyes. I felt like I had said something awful, and I was worried that she might cause a scene. It didn't come naturally to me to respond so directly to a girl. I expected a terrible reaction.

'What about grandpa?' She spoke.

I paused a bit and smirked, but she was expressionless and silent. I requested the man standing next to me to allow her, and surprisingly, I don't know why, all of them allowed her to go. They might have considered the urgency of the ladies-first type, I guess, as she was the only female there for sweets.

The shop owner packed her samosas, and she, in a rush, took the carry bag like she had a train to catch, glanced at me for milliseconds and smirked for a microsecond. A gentleman's courtesy, I would say, because I helped her.

About five minutes later, I had my samosa in my hand, and as I was about to devour it, my eye caught a vision that froze me for a moment.

That north-eastern girl was force-starting her scooty. It was a blood-red scooty. It looked like the battery was damaged, and the kick wasn't used for a long time, so the pedal got jammed.

The furious girl's face turned apple red. Her lean body was exhausted. A smile came upon my lips. She saw me. She felt a little insulted, but she galloped it. Her priority was to start the engine. She was inspecting it, and it was a sight to enjoy. It's something I've never seen before—a girl working as a mechanic at a railway crossing. I thoroughly enjoyed the sight, as I couldn't let my samosa get cold.

'Are you done?' I asked.

She stood up, put both of her hands on her waist, and didn't say a thing.

'I need an empty vessel or bottle and the tool kit,' I said.

Upon examining her bag, she handed me her water bottle. I retrieved the tool kit from the scooty's cabinet.

I loosened the bottom screw to get some engine oil into the bottle. Rubbed the oil onto the jammed kick pedal. I ensured gently that the kick pedal was fully lubricated. After the screw was tightened, I put the tool kit back.

'Kick it now,' I said.

She kicked, and the engine revved up. Putting on her helmet, she turned her attention towards me.

'You should've come sooner. My samosas got cold,' she said.

'You were supposed to thank me, Chinky.' My mind blurted.

'I was taking you as a mechanic, as you were almost in its engine,' I said.

'I was trying to fix its kick paddle,' she said.

The crossing barrier was lifted as the train passed by.

'**If you want to help someone, then help immediately, not when you find it comfortable**,' she said.

'What!' I exclaimed.

'Hadn't you come; I would've gone to the shop after the train.' She said and mentioned the shop next to the barricade.

'So, you…'

'And thanks!' She said finally.

She sped up her red scooty and vanished into the main market of Jwalapur.

I don't consider myself religious or atheist, but I do believe in faith and higher power. Faith has the power to bring out the goodness in people, which is exactly what we need right now. When you embrace faith, it's not about making God happy, whether you believe God is outside this world or exists invisibly within us. Instead, it's about finding happiness within yourself. That's how faith works – it brings inner peace and contentment. Just like all rivers flow into the ocean, all faiths and prayers lead to one ultimate source: the Creator.

We are born and we die. That's a fact. The time between birth and death is called life. Life is quite perplexing. We spend our whole lives trying to understand its meaning and how to make the most of it. We look to older generations for answers. I have searched countless times for a satisfying answer, but without success. So, I decided to stop searching and instead focus on observing one specific thing.

"It's not the death that is tragic, but what we let die inside of us while we live. —Norman Cousins."

I came to Haridwar to spend a few days with my little brother, who worked here in SIDKUL in an MNC, and it was my second day in this bustling city. Despite being younger, my brother possessed greater worldly knowledge and work experience compared to me. He was a completely practical person. He understood that in order to have a fulfilling life, he would need to make a living. There was no fictional universe in his mind. Motivated by my brother, I decided to step out of my comfort zone and uncover the fascinating wonders that Haridwar had to offer. I vowed to explore every nook and cranny. Although I have been to this city before, I want to fully immerse myself by exploring its streets without a specific plan– in various locations, at unpredictable times.

I was barefoot, and I started walking towards Arya Nagar Chowk, approximately 400m from Railway Faatak. The road leads you further into Haridwar. This is the market area, like any town could have. The furniture and electronics showrooms were recently opened a few years ago. Still, it wasn't very crowded.

I stopped at Arya Nagar Chowk near a police booth and walked towards the main road in the evening. I asked one person, and he told me to attend the Ganga Aarti at Har Ki Pauri.

'How far is it?'

'Fifteen minutes away.' He said and ignited the engine of his auto.

As we were heading towards the destination, the auto was being occupied by more people. The auto stopped at Shankar Ashram for a couple of minutes, where all its seats were occupied by commuters. I was in the back seat, and there were eight people inside it, plus two with the driver. He would've picked up four more passengers over the roof if it were allowed. I was suffocating. I couldn't sit for fifteen minutes.

'You can relax. It will be unoccupied in under five minutes. These are nearby people.' One man beside me was talking to another person. I was gazing upon the buildings and showrooms. I remembered Mohan Ji Poodi Wale restaurant as it was filling the surrounding with the aroma of *poodi*. The Red Chief showroom was there, and it reminded me I needed a pair of leather shoes.

After a couple of minutes, we reached Ranipur More, and three people got off. It was quite a relief.

An old song was being played by the driver. *Zindagi…. kaisi ye paheli…* Buses and autos take you to another time when you hear all the nostalgic songs and notice the lyrics that you haven't done before. I was lost for a couple of minutes. The auto stopped at the Rishikul Chowk, and now I was the only one besides the driver. Finally, I had it all by myself. There was a white Royal Enfield belonging to cops, and they were stopping the bike riders randomly for the challan.

The next stop was at the bus stand. Many people visit Haridwar for several reasons. The railway station was beside the bus stand. The essence of the Dharmnagri wasn't visible until I crossed the Laltharaav Bridge.

As I stood in Haridwar, I found myself immersed in the true essence of this holy city, renowned for its divine aura. The shops and stalls were antiquely showing the charisma of Dharmnagri. Copper and other metal utensils filled the shelves, alongside plastic flasks designed for carrying the sacred Ganga Jal. The vibrant melody of Ganga Aarti reverberated throughout the marketplace, filling my heart with a sense of profound spirituality. Sweet aroma of incense sticks wafted through the air. The saffron colour was abundant. Many people dressed in saffron clothes bearing mantras and symbols of religious significance. Some sages were smoking marijuana leaves through a clay pipe. Pulling its smoke inside with a brute force of lungs. It was truly a sight to behold and savour, a moment of transcendence and immersion in the mystical universe of Haridwar.

I was walking towards Har Ki Pauri. It took me fifteen minutes approximately, and I was at my destination. People were gathering for the Aarti. I stood over a bridge and carefully scanned the place as much as my eyes could. A clock tower stood nearby, manned by security personnel who were diligently monitoring the surroundings with their high-tech surveillance gadgets. I could see the highway, the opposite shore of the Ganga, and the VIP Ghat, all adding to the grandeur of the experience. A side view of a big splendid statue of Lord Shiva could be memorized beside the highway. I promised myself that I would go see this wondrous statue the next day. In the immediate vicinity, small temples dotted the landscape, with white square platforms lining the riverbank, ready for the sacred rituals of devout Hindus. Meanwhile, the gathering mob began to sing the Aarti, while a couple of men rang the bells repeatedly and swung trays filled with Diyaas and metallic lamps, adding to the splendour of the moment. Truly, it was a sight to behold, one that I would treasure in my heart for years to come.

The surrounding people were fully immersed in the moment. For nearly half an hour, they seemed to have shed all their worldly worries and surrendered themselves completely to the sacred ceremony unfolding before them. I received blessings from this holy place, and one purohit put a saffron tilak on my forehead. After the completion of the pious event, I decided to go back to my brother's place.

And here is the funny part. I'm always hungry. Though I ate those sweet samosas a couple of hours ago and I was starving again. I saw a dosa stall, and I got drawn to it. 'Stop bhaiya,' I said. I exclaimed to the auto driver, who looked at me quizzically, perhaps wondering why I was deviating from my intended destination. He stopped anyway. I ran towards the stall.

'At least pay me first, brother.' The auto driver yelled, as I had forgotten to pay him. I looked back.

Tapped on my head. 'Sorry, bhaiya.' I apologized and gave him ten rupees. I turned back towards the stall.

'Take your five back,' he said. I turned again. He smiled, as I was behaving like a hungry lion having hunted a sheep. I placed an order for a plain dosa. The man next to me was chewing loudly, which intensified my desire. I wanted my dosa before anyone, but I had to wait since people before me had already ordered. I looked around and there was Chitra Talkies, an old cinema behind the stall. The entrance was marked by two massive wooden doors, and the guard was seated there. It wasn't like the new multiplexes, it was a sight to behold, a reminder of a bygone era when grand theatres such as these were the cultural hub of the town. I stared at the big old hall, which was painted recently.

Out of nowhere, I noticed the red scooty parked there. The scooty looked identical, as the oil on the kick pedal was still present. I started looking for the owner and found her right beside me. The words sprouted out automatically.

'How come the world is too small?' I spoke. She gave me the same intense, chubby look.

'Haridwar is small.' She replied.

'Furious girl.' I blurted out.

'What does it mean?' She asked, as if I offended her.

'No, no, no... Don't take it wrong. People often take my words wrong, but my meaning and intentions always favour them,' I said.

'How,' she said.

'Well, it seems your brain is always in replying mode. You speak without even blinking. Too fast,' I said.

'Why am I not surprised?' She spoke as if this was a familiar statement to her.

'That's the thing I wanted to say. Look how fast you respond,' I said.

'Can I steal your place in the queue again? I'm in a hurry,' she said.

'You're always in a hurry,' I smirked and offered her my place.

Her broad forehead was more visible because of her tiny eyebrows. I started making assumptions. As I had observed her on two separate occasions, both times alone, it seemed apparent that she did not have many friends. Perhaps she was the only child, or maybe she simply preferred to keep to herself. But what struck me the most was the absence of a smile on her face, leading me to wonder if her parents had not provided her with the love and affection she needed. It was as if she was carrying the weight of the world on her shoulders, with deep secrets hidden behind her alluring facade.

'Don't you have any friends?' I asked.

She turned her face towards me and didn't reply. I felt bad. I shouldn't have asked her. The furious girl just lost her fury, and it pinched me.

'Why do you think I don't have friends?' She asked a couple of seconds later.

'Don't know, just for my curiosity,' I said.

Again, she didn't reply. Our turn had arrived, and we eagerly grabbed our freshly made dosas and retreated to our separate corners to enjoy the savoury meal. I couldn't help but notice how quickly she devoured her food, finishing her dosa in a matter of seconds. She then cleaned her hands with a napkin, took a quick sip of water, and made her way over to me.

'What are you exactly doing in Haridwar?' she asked.

'I'm a tourist, a sort of...a writer. Just came here to roam,' I said.

'Sort of writer? I've heard of writers, not a sort of writer,' she said.

'Well, I write provincial stories. The stories lie around us. I'm not someone like Shakespeare,' I said.

'I hate reading,' she said.

I gently touched my nose. It could have turned into an argument because I wanted to explain to her the importance of reading. However, I reminded myself of my teenage habits, where I would only study the night before an exam, so I shifted the subject.

'Do you have friends?' I asked.

'I do, but not in the way I want them to be.'

I smirked.

'Why are you smiling?' She asked.

'You need to learn a lot of things about friends.'

'I need to learn a lot of things about a lot of things. I know that.'

'Why don't you help me see this city? Just be my companion and we will learn a lot of things about a lot of things.'

'That sounds like a plan.'

'Yes, it is a plan.'

She turned on the engine of her scooty.

'If fate allows, and our paths cross again, I would gladly accompany you. Farewell, Mr. sort of writer,' she said and vanished into the crowded streets of Haridwar.

Chapter-2

Lord Shiva

I had promised myself the day before that I would visit that Lord Shiva's immense statue. So, I borrowed a bike. The time was 10 am, and I had recently finished my breakfast. My brother lived in Subhash Nagar, Jwalapur, and it's a densely populated place. Following my brother's suggestion, I decided to take the BHEL road. While passing through Swarn Jayanti Park, a police officer dressed in black signalled me to stop my motorcycle. I came to a halt. I had every document, so there should be nothing to worry about. It was an old Splendor motorcycle, but was in good condition. He asked me to show him the latest pollution certificate; it came as a blow. I never knew that bikes should have a pollution certificate, too. It was for four-wheelers I had presumed! My day thus started with a Rs.500 fine. Later, the cop advised me to get the pollution levels checked for the bike at a nearby petrol pump to prevent further problems. Upon seeing the map, I discovered the closest petrol pump was at Ranipur More. I went through the procedure, and while the man was printing out the paper, I saw the red scooty again. Her mother was with her, so she was not alone. She inherited the nose and eyes from her mother. She looked at me and I was about to wave at her, but I didn't.

'Maybe next time.' I thought.

I saw her going. For a couple of seconds, I thought I could follow her, but my well-wisher mind discouraged me at the nick of the moment.

'If it's meant to be, it will be.' I thought again.

I moved towards my destination. Upon taking the right at the crossroads, I followed the road that led to the Prem Nagar Ganga bridge. I stopped for a while, stood over the bridge, and started observing the panorama. It was fabulous— a thousand gallons of water was just passing beneath my feet. As I was staring deep, it felt like the water was stationary and the bridge was moving. My head started reeling, giving me a hangover-like feeling. I widened my arms in the famous titanic posture for a couple of seconds. I stared at the green, artificial grass-covered logo that read, 'I love Haridwar.' The weather was absolutely fine since the summer had gone. A cold breeze was nourishing my skin, and it was force-stopping me. A couple of people were at the Ghat before my eyes. I didn't know the name of the Ghat, so I decided to search for all the Ghat's names after visiting the statue. There was a pathway beside the river for those who love to walk. It felt like walking in heaven. How come a person wouldn't enjoy the walk beside the divine Ganga River?

I headed towards the statue. I was on the highway cruising at leisurely 40 km per hour. There was a tonne of hotels on my right, and the pathway was on my left. I was driving at my own wonderful pace. While I was lost in my thoughts, a beautiful sight just made me gasp. I halted and saw that beautifully constructed 'Om'. My eyes did some research and found out that it was a Ghat too—Amrapur Ghat. There was a path going inside from Amrapur Ghat, which on the left side leads into the Bus Stand and on the right-side leads to another Ghat near a guest house. And there was that Om bridge. A cuboidal duct was fastened to the metallic wires in a circle's segment shape. The duct resulted in the finishing part of our holy symbol 'Om', which was extremely gorgeous. It was a perfect white-coloured spiritual symbol. Haridwar didn't cease to surprise me.

I arrived at the Chandighat Bridge Chowk. On my right, there was a long highway bridge. The name Chandighat was because it pays homage to the Goddess Chandi Devi. The temple can be seen with an upward glance. It is the connecting bridge that leads the way there. The temple is on the top of the mountain, and one has to climb there to get the blessings, or you could go via rope elevators, i.e., *Udan Khatola*. The bridge is almost one kilometre. That vital highway connects Haridwar to Najibabad, which was another route to enter Uttar Pradesh.

On my left, the intercity road leads to the road connected to Har Ki Pauri, but I had to go straight on the Haridwar-Rishikesh highway. I sped up and saw a barrage on my right and a road which goes inside it. I marked it for my next assessment and one more small bridge to cross, and here I was, confronting the statue, the marvellous huge art. The beautiful and divine Lord Shiva. The dazzling blue-coloured physique with a golden 'Trishul' in the left hand. The right hand was offering blessings to the universe, where the bicep was coiled by a snake. Two Rudraksha necklaces were long and lying up to the abdomen. The fully grown cobra snake possesses its own distinct charm. It covered the lower neck and chest portion and was skilfully crafted with beautiful carvings. The cobra's fierce expression and visible tongue lent an air of aggression. The hair was matted and knotted, and the braid styled to resemble a mountain over the head, providing a masculine dazzled look. The braid peak was wrapped around by another snake. The waxing crescent phase moon nested over the forehead seems to be attracting the powers of the entire universe. The torso was covered in saffron cloth with black spots on it. It resembled cheetah skin and covered the area from the abdomen to the shoulder. It was a pause-worthy moment, and I was submerged in it. The Lord was smiling like he wanted me to say that now all your problems had vanished. I was lost in the Shiva Universe, the mythology we have been hearing since our birth. Holding the poison into his throat, the third destructive eye, and the Tandava. I was visualizing everything; my brain was unearthing the childhood television memory of Lord Shiva. I sought refuge in his shelter. It brought me joy, and once I had taken a plethora of pictures, I headed back to my room.

I was laying down in my bed and somehow, the statue was revolving inside my head. I was in the sort of "Lord Shiva hangover". It was cold, so I stood up to prepare a cup of tea. I was standing beside the stove and scrolling random videos on YouTube and there I saw the ad of a scooty, the red scooty, and my mind hammered me to remember her.

'Maybe I could see her tomorrow, isn't it, my lord?' I was praying to Shiva.

The boiling tea stole my focus. I poured it into my cup and just watched the entire ad of that scooty. The digital meter, the combi brake, and the mileage, all I was focused on was its red colour. It was a day full of discoveries to keep my mind in a beautiful state.

I was reading a renowned author Khaled Husseini book, and that book hooked me so well for two days. On the very third day, I didn't have that bike, so I was in an auto. Before Ranipur More, I saw a restaurant named The Pizza Castle. The hunger made me stop. I went inside and it was a regular restaurant. I sat there and ordered one onion pizza with extra cheese and a coke. The restaurant had a pleasant atmosphere, with instrumental music providing a soothing background ambiance. A couple in the corner seat was having some disagreement over chowmeen. The lady wanted to scream, but the man was in a stable state, helping the restaurant maintain its peace. All of a sudden, three girls came into that restaurant and occupied the seat facing my back. I didn't see their faces, but two of them were teasing the third. They were in their teens. My attention was soon refocused on my delicious pizza. One girl went to the reception and ordered one sweet corn pizza, white pasta, and momos. She later came back to order one coke, which I forgot to collect from the counter. As I went to retrieve my drink, I turned around and found myself face-to-face with the red scooty girl, who was sitting and staring at me intently like I was about to be banished from that place. I smiled and rushed back to my chair.

'All hail to lord shiva.' I said to myself.

Suddenly, the teasing stopped, and the murmuring started. Now, they were into something serious or maybe a sudden phobia of their class test or exam took them over. I didn't turn around to see her, but I did know that she will be thinking about me and the promise she made. I was expecting to have a few words of chit-chat with her. Maybe it was Lord Shiva's blessing. My eating pace has significantly decreased, and my salivary glands are not producing sufficient saliva to facilitate rapid pizza consumption. I was chewing and thanks to coke which was the pusher there, otherwise I wouldn't be able to swallow it. I was waiting for the moment that she would come to me or all three of them would say hello. None of this happened. The moment I was going to finish my last piece, they stood up and left the place.

'Maybe Lord Shiva wants me to wait for more.' I thought.

I came outside and crossed the road as I was planning to visit more Ghats that day. I researched the Ghat, which I was watching from the Prem Nagar bridge. It was called Govind Ghat. I waved at one auto, and like always, it was full. I asked for the Govind Ghat and the driver said he would leave me at the S. M. J. N College Chowk, from where I had to walk about one kilometre.

'Okay,' I said.

I suddenly noticed that someone was honking at me. As I turned over, there she was once again.

With a grin on her face, she was scanning me.

'Tell him to go,' she said to me.

It took a few seconds to process who she was referring to, and with sudden reflexes I told the auto driver to go.

'You came,' I said to make a conversation.

'So, where to, Mr. Sort of writer?'

'To Govind Ghat.'

'Okay, drive.'

'Are you comfortable if I drive?'

'Can't you?'

'I would, means I will, okay, just give me the helmet.'

'You won't need it here. Just do as I say.'

I took over and started driving.

'So, you came back after a long thought process, didn't you?' I asked.

'No, I had to leave them at their tuition.'

'What if you didn't make it here on time?'

'You don't eat, you just pick. I knew I would catch you.'

'What if…'

'Turn right,' she intervened.

'Okay,' I turned right towards the S. M. J. N College.

'You were asking something,' she said.

'What if you didn't make it?' I asked.

'Today I had to,'

'Impressive,'

'I saw you that day, at the petrol pump. My mum and I were together.'

'I saw you too.'

'That day I decided I would keep my promise the next time.'

'Okay,' I stretched for a long.

'That's why I didn't miss today.'

'Park it here under that oak tree,' she said.

I parked it where she suggested and we entered the parameter of the Govind Ghat. The floor was covered with saffron-coloured tiles. There was a temple just near the entrance, and benches were provided across the Ghat to sit. It was perfectly suitable for evening and morning walks and sit-chatting. We grabbed one bench.

Some of the college students were roaming there.

'They bunk their classes to come here,' she said.

'Beautiful reason to bunk. I would gladly spend my time here to avoid boring classes. Just to feel the coolness here,' I said.

'We often come here,' she said.

'Oh, means your friends, I guess,' I said.

'Yeah,' she said in a low voice, lowering her head.

'You don't seem to enjoy them.'

She didn't answer this.

'God, I touched the wrong nerve.' I scolded myself.

'How are your friends?' She asked a couple of seconds later while I was scolding myself.

'The...They're fine, I guess...actually they are fine,' I replied hesitantly.

'You guess? Don't you talk to them daily?' She asked.

'What! Why would I talk to them daily?' I said.

'You should. They're your friends, and friends are our chosen families and we should take care of each other,' she said.

'Yes, but that doesn't mean that we should call them every day.'

'Then how would you ensure they are okay?'

I bit my lower lip. I got muted into my mind.

'Was I into another world when I was a teenager? I never thought like that.' I asked myself.

'Look, we don't need to babysit our friends. We are already connected by invisible wires. This time my friends would be working and they would be thinking the same for me. We don't need to tell each other every day how our day was,' I said.

'I call them every day, despite that. It's always doubtful to me if they are truly my genuine friends,' she said.

'Sometimes they get irritated while talking to me over the phone,' she said further.

'And how much time do you spend over the phone every day?' I asked.

'Sometimes it's less than two minutes if arguments start in the beginning, otherwise, it lasts up to hours,' she said.

'When talks and meetings take place in school during the day, then what is the point of talking on the phone for two hours afterwards?' I asked.

'It feels like compulsion, like if I won't talk to them, they will leave me,' she asked.

'Could you tell me about your friends? About their behaviour, food habits, and nature?' I asked.

'Yes, I can. One of them is…'

'No need right now, but when you meet them next time, just ask them if they could tell you the same stuff about you,' I intervened.

'What does that mean?'

'I will tell you when you do it.'

'Today is my lucky day. Lord Shiva blessed me more than I could ask for,' I said further.

'Why? Because of me?'

'I won't lie. I love to connect to the incomplete and broken people.'

'Am I incomplete or broken?'

'Right now, you're curious and furious.'

'Please tell me, please…please.'

'I will…just do what I've said.'

As the wind carried the aroma of incense sticks, I savoured the moment, immersed in the soothing atmosphere. The Ganga flowed with an unblemished aura of serenity and purity, inviting me to lose myself in its beauty. However, my trance was interrupted when she asked for my phone number.

We exchanged our contact numbers.

'I hope writers use WhatsApp,' she said.

'Yes, but I prefer calling over chatting.'

'I expected you would say such a thing.'

'Are you leaving?' I asked.

'Yes, I'm a teenager and I have some restrictions.'

'So, today's quota of roaming is over for you.'

'Yes, we'll go to Chilla. Next time, you'd love it.'

'Okay, sure.'

'Could I drop you somewhere?'

'I want to sit here; I will go by myself.'

'Okay then, bye Mr. Writer.'

When she left, I thought of my life without friends. I tried to push my mind if there was a day in my life when I had to endure such a solitary existence. I didn't find any. My friends have been an ever-present force in my life. Although our interactions have diminished, I still believe that they are with me, always. This girl was trying to run her friendship forcibly, and that's impossible. I saw a young and beautiful couple where the boy was tenderly combing the girl's hair as she blushed with delight. A pious priest busily prepared a plethora of incense sticks, their fragrant aroma filling the air. Whenever I wanted to leave my seat, the breeze restrained me. People were calm. I turned to my left side and found a thin road alongside the river. I took a walk, and there was a colony of slums and makeshift homes.

'What a fabulous place you have chosen.' I commented.

As I made my way through the slum colony, I hailed an auto and embarked on my journey homeward. I checked my phone and there were notifications. I allow no app to show notifications except WhatsApp, calls, and messages. There were two text messages from an unknown number.

'Hello, Mr. Writer?' and *'Where are you? Don't you check your messages?'*

Now, my WhatsApp had twenty messages, which was a completely shocking thing. This was an uncommon occurrence, as I am well-known for my delayed responses on WhatsApp. Most people who know me opt to communicate via call.

I read them — from the same number. The first ten messages were sent within fifteen minutes asking where I was. The next two messages were two ignoring emojis, the next two were angry emojis, and then the next six messages were compelling me to text her back immediately, like she had very important things to tell. I had my read receipt feature off. Once I changed my clothes, I ate my lunch. I was watching Breaking Bad at that time when Walter White just started to enjoy his skill, and I was completely into it. My phone rang, and I picked it up.

'Why can't you reply immediately to some broken people?' She asked.

'Just arrived,' I defended myself.

'I did what you asked me to do.'

'So, what did you get?'

'They don't know me, they are just using me,' she said in a crumpled voice.

'Now, that's a terrible situation.' I thought.

'Because you never let them know you,' I said.

'I don't know, and that's hurting. You were right, I'm alone.'

'Listen, you don't need to—'

'Most terrible thing is that they do know each other very well,' she intervened.

'Listen, just make some space. Don't punch yourself,' I said.

'Can we meet tomorrow?' She asked.

I thought for a long time and asked her to come to Swarn Jayanti Park at 10 am. She agreed.

Chapter-3

The Wanderers

She arrived punctually. I was driving, and she was my navigator. At Chandighat Chowk, she told me to take the right on the bridge. It was the same one-kilometre-long Chandighat Bridge.

'Just look at the peak of the mountain,' she told me.

I looked and there was a temple over the mountain.

'It's the Chandi Devi temple,' she said.

Then I tried to solve the map inside my head because when I was at Har Ki Pauri, I gazed upon both mountain temples, Chandi Devi and Mansa Devi. My mind raced as I attempted to map out the routes in my head, scanning the roadmap of Haridwar with intense focus. When the bridge finished, we turned left. The right one was leading to Kotdwar, Najibabad. Five minutes later, we approached the entrance gate of Chandi Devi.

'This is the trekking route to the temple, which takes nearly forty-five minutes, as I heard,' she said.

I stopped the scooty and watched the massive bell at the entrance.

'Don't stop, you could visit some other day here, just drive,' she said.

Now we were in the forest area of Rajaji National Park, Chilla Range. The road we travelled upon was a thing of beauty, with towering trees lining both sides of the path, casting shadows over us. The chill of winter hung in the air, enlivening my senses and causing my skin to tingle with each gust of breeze. We soon came upon a checkpoint where forest officers resided in a large and imposing structure. Several safari jeeps were parked nearby, beckoning to tourists such as ourselves who wished to immerse themselves in the captivating jungle. Despite our excitement, my companion and I remained silent observers, taking in the surroundings with a sense of reverence and awe.

As we continued on our journey, we came upon a truly stunning sight: a magnificent barrage that took my breath away. The sheer beauty of its construction was enough to compel me to park our scooty under a nearby tree so that we could stand upon the bridge and take in the full splendour of the sight.

Water cascaded down from different chambers of turbines, creating a mesmerizing display of natural power and beauty. The canal's side area was adorned with exquisite stonework and intricate wall paintings. She stood beside me, equally awed by the sight before us. It was a moment of pure wonder and appreciation for the natural world, one that we were grateful to experience and savour.

'You seem to be so busy with yourself,' she said.

I, who was lost in the flora and fauna, suddenly woke up.

'I never came here; shouldn't I get lost in such a beautiful panorama?' I spoke.

'Okay, just tell me when you're done,' she said and grabbed her phone in her hand. She wasn't enjoying my company and suddenly, I became too boring for her little curious and furious mind.

'One day you will understand this,' I said.

'Huh-uh,' she replied uninterestedly.

'You were babysitting your friends. That's why they don't know you as you know them,' I said.

Her fingers, which were typing something, stopped.

'What did you say?'

'Don't be their mother, just be a comrade,' I said.

'A comrade?'

'Amm…like soldiers. Do you know how soldiers live with each other?'

Her curious face was expecting an immediate reply.

'Okay, they drink and laugh with each other when they get the free time. They work when they are at work and they work as a team when they are at battle or war,' I said.

'So, what do I conclude?'

'Just be original, do your stuff as they do. Build yourself and let them get to know you. Don't just wait for their call to pick up and drop them off. Learn to say no. You don't have to call them every day.'

'Friendship grows best with the least effort. It's a daily phenomenon and you don't have to do anything special for it,' I said.

'But if I stopped calling them, it would ruin everything.'

'Then you don't have to be somewhere where you don't belong.'

'I fear of being alone.'

'It would be better to be alone than to be in strange company.'

She swiped her phone screen and showed me a photo of a forty-year-old handsome man.

'Your father?' I guessed.

'Yes.' She said and swiped a couple of more times on the screen and showed me a second photo of the same man but in a terrible and unhealthy condition. The body was pale white and swollen.

I didn't speak.

'You could guess again,' she said.

Then I realized the emotional trauma she was hiding under her skin.

'You didn't tell me that your father is sick. All you were doing was blah-blahing about your friends,' I said.

'Now you can understand why I'm afraid of being alone.'

'No, I didn't.'

'How could I? You were supposed to be discussing your father rather than your friends.'

'I'm angry with my father. He never listened to anyone, and now, we are all bearing because of him. There is complete disarray in my family. My mother is fully occupied with keeping him alive. My brother is only eight,' she said.

'And instead of paying attention to your family, you're thinking about your friends,' I said.

'What should I do?' She asked. Her face suddenly peeled off.

I felt pity for her. She was totally in a dilemma.

'Why are you struggling so much?' I asked.

'I don't understand.'

'Okay, I know you're suffering, but why are you extending your suffering by putting yourself among those idiots?'

She remained silent.

'If any part of our body gets a single wound, then the whole body feels its pain. Family is the same. If one member is suffering, then everyone else is suffering too. Don't seek your emotional settlement outside. If you're at peace at home, then every relationship will be automatically taken care of,' I justified.

We were standing on the bridge and facing the barrage. She was extremely silent, and that was shocking because I wanted her to say something. I looked at her. Her eyelids were stationary, like something deep had caught her. Unexpectedly, she turned towards me and put on a fake smile.

'Are you hungry?' I asked.

She nodded her head negatively, then she said something.

'I don't know what to do. The girls of my age are happy. They are complete and they have almost everything. They spend their day normally, living with their parents. Having their secret boyfriends and chat buddies. And I wake up and check if my father is sleeping or aching with pain. My mother sometimes forgets about us; she gets tired and forgets to feed her son. I'm taking care of my brother as a mother. Every time I see a normal family, my heart cries. I don't know what to do,' she said, in a crumbled voice.

'I understand. We always seek what we don't have,' I said.

'I want redemption from this miserable destiny. I want to be free like others,' she said.

'But that's not upon us. There are some terrible mistakes I've made in my past that I wish I could erase from memory. A few of them were absolutely terrible and made in a desperate state of mind. Although they are irreversible, I am still affected by those. Whatever decision you take, remember, *karma* will never leave you,' I said.

'Can you mention one mistake, particularly?' She asked.

I looked at her and then gazed upon a calf grazing beside the bridge.

'In an act of rebellion, I left my home, fuelled by a desire to see my parents in pain. My intention was to hurt them on purpose, and the impact was so deep that I still can't make it right. Despite everything, my mother still fears losing me whenever I go somewhere. She doesn't trust me, and I wish I could make up for this mistake,' I said.

'You can control the actions, not the consequences,' I said further. She nodded her head.

'What do you want me to do?' She asked.

'Just prioritize important things,' I said.

'I'm a teenager. I don't know how to do that. I just crave for things and sometimes I crave so badly.'

'For me, family is the final destination. No matter what you do, or what you achieve, at the end of the day, everyone wants to be with their family. If we are distant, then we miss them. Nothing is above the love of the family. You should start considering that.'

'When it comes to loving my mom, she thinks of me as stone-hearted, that I don't have emotions. I'm a terrible person.'

'No one is super solved. We are what we are, sometimes confused, sometimes evolved, and sometimes destroyed...nothing else.'

She remained silent for a couple of minutes. 'Let's go to one more place,' she said.

'That would be great,' I said.

We caught the road going parallel to the canal. It was one of the most beautiful roads I've ever seen. The left side was the Rajaji National Park's jungle area, and on the right side was the beautiful canal.

'Where does this road lead?' I asked.

'Rishikesh.'

'So, are we going to Rishikesh?'

'Nope, I have time constraints. There is a place in this forest.'

Nearly after twenty minutes, she asked me to take a left. A semi-concrete, ungraded road was leading us into the depth of the forest. We crossed a small village. The village seemed to be unchanged for centuries. A few ladies were carrying grass bundles over their heads for livestock. The distinct odour of dung and farm animals was forcing me to look back into my childhood, when my grandpa used to do these chores for our cows and buffaloes. Some houses were still mud houses having thatch as a roof. Children were playing cricket near a primary school. The banks of the roads were decorated with small stones, giving the village an antiquated feel. She kept saying to move ahead. We were encountering the dense shadows of enormous trees. A known spicy fragrance permeated my nostrils, and I saw a little garden of curry leaves. I wished to pluck a few leaves but time was short. A temple came after a few hundred meters.

'You want to take me here? I didn't think of you as a religious person,' I said.

'Come with me,' she said.

We didn't enter the temple. We passed beside it, and the next thing I saw just blew my mind. It was a field of stones, pebbles, and sand.

The Ganga River was flowing among them in almost parallel streams. It was a wide area as far as my eyes could see. The sun's rays were reflected in the water, giving it a silver coating. In the ultimate calm place, all you can hear was nature: the flowing water, the birds, and nothing else. On the other side of the river, I saw two Sambhar grazing. I followed her. She took me to a broken tree that was lying in the sand. This tree came here by flowing with the stream. Half buried in the sand and half sticking out. She asked me to sit on the branch beside her. A soft breeze was comforting her hair and providing a gentle swing.

With a face full of natural happiness, I sat there. I was just smiling for no reason. I was in the best place. My soul was speaking to me.

'How come I never came here before? I will never forget this place,' I said.

'I'm glad you liked it.'

Our eyes locked for a couple of seconds, then she started looking at the river.

'You are still not happy,' I said.

'I'm trying.'

'Just don't lose whatever is in your hand, don't let your present regret your future. Just be that furious girl which I met that day.'

And finally, she smiled.

'When I was fixing my scooter that day, you were enjoying the view, right?' She asked.

I chuckled.

'That was a rare sight. I couldn't miss.'

'It feels awkward when someone notices your inability.'

'At least you were trying. Girls rarely look into the engines.'

'And... where do girls look into?' She asked, picking on me.

I looked at her. Her head was down and wrinkles were formed around the corner of her eyes, showing that she was blushing.

'I don't know exactly, but they don't look into engines normally,' I said.

'Where do you live in Haridwar exactly?' I asked.

'Shastri Nagar, Jwalapur.'

'I want to see the towns of Haridwar.'

'You're most welcome to my town.'

'Can you teach me any of my board subjects?' She asked further.

'I can, but I'm not here for much time, maybe for a couple of days or a week.'

'Then it would be like a crash course.'

I grinned.

'I will come with one of my friends, and we will pay you.'

'Why are you insisting?'

'Please,' she pleaded. Through her use of the word "please," she expressed her strong longing for someone to genuinely hear and understand her.

'Okay, don't pay me, but we could visit one more place,' I said.

'Sure,' she said.

'I'm a morning person. You have to come before 9 am,' I said.

She intensely gazed upon my face, and after long processing, replied affirmatively.

'Okay then, see you tomorrow,' I said.

Chapter-4

Lost and Found

'The chemistry must not be disrespected,' said Walter White to the idiot Jesse Pinkman, who was just a drug freak and dumb. I was looking into some previous episodes of Breaking Bad.

It was time for me to have my coffee. It was midnight, and my brother was loudly snoring. His constant complaints about lack of sleep because of his job were nothing but a big lie. At exactly 11 pm, I witnessed him snoring soundly in bed, and he typically woke up at 8 am.

Nine hours of sleep! And still complaining. That's because of the unjustified and unsatisfying job. An unsatisfying job is always energy-sucking. All you want is to escape, and that's why your brain demands more sleep just because you don't want to work.

As my brother left, I heard the bell. I opened the door and two girls were standing there, and I almost forgot that I said something to someone the day before! I paused for a couple of seconds because my room wasn't in a state to allow two strangers even to inspect. It wasn't broomed properly.

'Morning person! I thought you would be awake by 4 am, and burying your head into some book by now,' she said.

'It is what it is.' I giggled and let them in.

'Make yourselves comfortable,' I said.

The other girl wasn't happy at all. It was difficult to process what she was saying as she mumbled into her ears. To keep her cool, she waved her hand.

My room had a big Deadpool poster in which one of his hands was on his butt and the other one was shushing the audience, labelled as 'Hard ass, Smart ass, Deadpool.' The rest of the room was barren. There were two books and several pairs of my clothes in the doorless concrete closet, and a charger was plugged in.

I asked them to wait for a couple of minutes.

I removed the dirty utensils, torn Maggi packets, chips packets, and Coke bottle. I arranged a table and two chairs from my brother's room.

I was sitting on my bed with my legs dangling and there was a table in front of me and both of them were sitting on the other side of the table.

'So, what do you want to learn?' I asked.

'We want to learn about anything outside our syllabus,' she said.

'That's not a good time for a joke.'

'We already have enough tuitions. We came here just for nothing, or anything that could be other than usual,' she said.

'You could've slept for one or more hours if you didn't want to study,' I said.

'Why is everyone and everything around us so consumed with our studies? We are engrossed in this foolish idea of studying from the moment the sun rises till the moon yawns. There is no time to relax,' the other girl said.

I noticed a handbook that belonged to the other girl, and it had the name 'Neetu' imprinted on it. Just as I was about to see her full name on her textbook, she quickly placed her palm over it. Until that moment, we hadn't yet exchanged our names.

'Yes, because it's necessary, knowledge is the only tool that paves the path to the future,' I said.

'A few of us will go to the best institutions, and the rest will look for one here and there,' she said.

'All animals in the jungle can't climb trees, nor can all swim or fly. We are what we are,' I said.

'That's why we came to you,' she said.

'I don't know why you're here because if you want me to sing a song for you or to tell you a story, that's not me, neither I'm a philosopher,' I said.

'Just tell us anything good. We are not here to pass the time; we are here to utilize it,' she said.

'Don't you have your...male friends?' I asked.

'Boyfriends,' she completed it.

'No, don't you have someone in your life?' She asked to me.

I looked at her inspecting eyes. Those tiny, curious eyes were compelling me to reveal anything to her. That expression of hers was a replica of some TV show where the actress seduces an actor through her eyes. I was almost submerged into them.

'If I'm to be your tutor, then we can't deviate from our goals. It is best not to inquire about such things,' I said.

'Please, we want some air from the words, some dopamine. At least you could spare us from these Cos theta and Calculus stuff,' she said.

It turns out they were right. Conversations about the board exams and related syllabus topics were mentally draining. There must be some discussions beyond the syllabus. As the other girl said, 'some dopamine'.

'I had,' I said.

'What happened then? Break up?' She asked.

'Or she got married to some other guy against her will.' Neetu said and laughed.

'How could someone get married against his or her will?' I asked her.

'Where patriarchy prevails,' she said.

'Imagine if your mother refused to marry your father, then we wouldn't be having this conversation right now,' I said.

'That was a different time,' she said.

'Even so, she accepted the marriage, and here you are,' I said.

'But I hate arranged marriages,' she said.

'Marriage is a social system. Love is a gift from nature. A marriage can be drawn from love, but vice versa is a matter of luck. Back then, elders made all the decisions for their children. They bind the couple with responsibilities first, and thus their marriages worked. In my opinion, whether it is a love marriage or arrange, acceptance of the marriage matters,' I said.

Neetu nodded her head affirmatively.

'How does it feel when someone breaks up with another?' She asked.

'It's like someone has torn your heart. Suddenly, you have all the reasons to curse this world. For me, it was like someone from my family…died and…he won't come back ever,' I said.

'So, you never met her after the breakup?' She asked.

'How could you meet someone who is dead to you? That person won't be the one you used to meet…you could just miss that person,' I said.

'But people break up and then patch up and break up again and so on…'

'A relationship is not a game. When you commit to someone, either you're in or you're out; there is no middle way. And being committed to someone is a very dangerous decision. It affects everything in your life, the whole routine. It makes you strong and vulnerable both at the same time,' I said.

'Your generation is too messy,' I said further.

'You're talking like our parents,' Neetu said.

'I'm talking facts. Most of your generation's mood depends upon gadgets. A single message either could make your day or worsen your day. Your relationships work on Instagram. I'm not much elder than you but still there is a lot of difference between today and ten years ago,' I said.

'But it's social media, it connects us,' she said.

'Yes, it connects us, but it should not affect us. It shouldn't be able to steal our focus or swing our mood,' I said.

'I can't imagine a life without Instagram and Snapchat,' Neetu said.

'You should start. You should learn to miss a person having your eyes closed rather than stalking his profile or reading old messages.'

'I will shut off Instagram. It really consumes a lot of my time,' she said.

'Don't shut off, just hide the notifications first. Your account should exist but, in the way, as you own it, not as it owns you.'

'Connect to people occasionally. The less a person is bound by restrictions and relations, the more he will be capable of doing something extraordinary.'

'I never expected you to be a counsellor,' Neetu said.

'No, I'm not. If some of my things are really going to influence you, then I want to assure you of these things first.' I said further.

'Okay, that's all for today,' I finished.

'We will come tomorrow,' Tanu said.

'Text me first,' I said.

That's something teenagers typically do. They seek questions. Now that they have entered the real world but are reluctant to fully embrace it. They wanted to be lost and get found. Any strange event happening around them creates a questionnaire for them.

Until now, she had been like a maze, and she wanted me to help her find her way. But how could I make it happen?

She called me Mr. Writer, and for me, she was a red scooty chinky girl. We didn't share our names. I was just about to type a message to know her name and, in the meantime, she called me.

'Want to go somewhere? Our tuition teacher is absent,' she asked.

'Someone is seizing the opportunity, huh?' I said.

'Just tell me,' she said.

'Come,' I said.

She came within ten minutes. And, like always, gave me the keys.

'I tasted no non-veg, but I always wanted to. My father used to eat, but my mother never allowed me to go to him. There is a biryani shop near my home. Its spicy smell drove me crazy every time I passed by. Would you…please?' She said.

'But why didn't you go with your friends?' I asked.

'They are vegetarians and they judge,' she said while pouting her lips.

I smiled.

'Well, they don't judge you. It's the food,' I said.

'They won't eat with me if I tell them I eat chicken,' she said.

'Then don't. Maybe someday, they will stop judging, or eventually, they will start eating too,' I said.

I ordered a half-plate biryani for her, and within minutes, she ate all of it. She ate the pieces of chicken like she has been devouring them for a lifetime.

'How's your father?' I asked.

She, licking her submerged fingers in the ghee and spices, paused for a second, stared at me, and resumed licking.

'He doesn't want to be fine,' she said.

'Everyone wants to be fine,' I said.

'You won't understand,' she said.

Her reply stopped me from asking further questions about her father.

'I would like to visit your home,' I asked.

'Sure,' she said, while cleaning her fingers with a tissue.

'Now,' I said.

She paused.

'Now is not the correct time. We will, someday,' she said.

I offered, 'If you allow me to visit now, I can be your tutor for any subject you prefer.'

She gave me a quick glance.

'That means my tutor wants to visit my home.'

'Well, that would be fine for my mother,' she added.

I drove the scooty to Shastri Nagar, Jwalapur. The town was crowded, as it contained almost half the population of the city. The whole Jwalapur was divided into sub-towns, and Shastri Nagar was one of them. I almost turned ten times, and I'm too weak to remember the routes. I was sure that I could never find that house alone. It was like a maze, one route leading to another sub-town or crossroad.

A youngster, around ten years old, was looking at us, ready to do something mischievous, like hurl a water-filled balloon at us. His face had a healthy and youthful appearance because of his round and rosy cheeks.

'That's my brother,' she said.

'His eyes are completely normal,' I blurted out.

'And mine are almost hidden,' she said.

'That's not what I meant,' I said, smiling a bit.

'That's okay, I'm used to it. Let's go inside,' she said.

We went inside.

Whenever I enter a new house, my attention is immediately drawn to the way items are arranged, as it is a skill I have been eager to cultivate for quite some time. Throughout my life, my room has consistently been in a state of disarray. The house was impeccably maintained, showing great care and attention to detail.

I witnessed her mother tending to her sick father, administering medication to him.

'Meet my new tuition teacher, Maa, he will teach me…'

'Physics.'

'Maths.'

We both blurted out.

Her mother paused and looked at both of us.

'I mean both,' I corrected her.

She stared at me.

'Namaste Ji,' I greeted both of them by joining my hands.

'Please, have a seat,' her mother said.

I sat on a stool in their living room, which was on the first floor. The ground floor belonged to her uncle. Her aunt was monitoring me through the channel window.

I also gave her aunt a greeting. With a grin, she turned back.

She asked me to come to her study room. I walked inside. In the study room, there was a coffee-coloured study table and a matching coffee-coloured shelf, complemented by a stunning orange painted wall adorned with a beautiful family collage.

'Tanu,' her mother cried out a name.

'Coming,' she replied.

'Tanu,' I said, raising my eyebrows.

She smiled.

'Thanks to your mother,' I said.

'I knew today you will know my name,' she said.

As her mother called her, she served us tea along with freshly prepared namkeen. The roasted *chana*, white murmure, roasted peanuts, almonds, cashews, and tiny bits of walnut blended with the aalu bhujia were a flavourful and delicate mix. It was a stylish and healthful little snack. I was enticed to take a cup of the tea merely by its colour and scent.

We sat in her room, and I was searching for cashews in the namkeen, and a few minutes later, her mother hopped in.

'Tanu told me briefly about you,' her mother said.

My hand stopped searching, and I picked whatever I got in a hurry and gulped it into my mouth.

'She told me about you and her father, too. You have a very nice, well-arranged, beautiful home,' I said.

'But the person who built this isn't aware of his achievements,' she said, while mentioning her father. For a while, she was again in sorrow, but she hid it, wiped her eyes with the *dupatta* of her green-striped suit.

'How much is your fee? I can't afford more than a thousand rupees,' she said, putting the deadlines.

'It's okay, fine,' I said, to minimize her worry.

'You are a strong woman, it's amazing for me how you are taking care of all the things, parallelly,' I said.

'Who else will?' She replied.

And she is right.

'Okay then, call me if she doesn't behave accordingly. I have to feed her father,' she said and stood up.

'Don't worry,' I said.

'Bring him the sweets and feed his contact number into my phone,' she said to Tanu and moved towards her father's room.

'Is it okay if I meet your father?' I asked.

'But he won't welcome you, he is…you know,' she said.

'Okay, let's go then, drop me,' I said.

'Let's go.' As she spoke, we made our way over to the scooty.

As I was driving the scooty, a list of things was making hustle and bustle in my mind. A lot of *hows* and *whys*. I was silent. She was quiet, too. She was only instructing me where to turn. I stopped the scooty at a juice shop.

'Banana Shake?' I asked her.

'Oreo,' she said.

Her face turned again to a one-word-answer girl. Actually, she had things to think about. Her mother was occupied twenty-four hours, and she was the eldest child.

'My granny turned every stone, visited almost every famous temple, dargah, called babas and hakims, but no one has that power to make my father healthy. I gave up on all the superstitions,' she said.

'When beliefs shatter, the world becomes hell.'

The shop owner gave her the Oreo shake.

'Why are you silent?' She asked.

'Why are you staring at me? You are scaring me,' she said further.

She shook my hand. I came back from a short coma. I looked around.

'Sorry, I was lost,' I said.

I picked up my pineapple juice.

'Where were you? What were you thinking?' She asked.

'Finish your shake first,' I said.

'Can't we talk like that?' She asked.

'Okay, so, Tanu, it's time to accept the reality. Your mother has shown faith in me. It's my sole responsibility now that I must teach you. I can't stand deceiving her,' I said.

'She just wants me to be occupied and, sure, you can teach me,' she said.

'She understood!! Wow!!'

'From tomorrow, just come on time'.

Chapter-5

Escaping the Reality

The next day, both of them came on time. I was ready too. I had sprayed a room freshener and had cleaned my entire room.

'Let's hurry,' I said.

I opened her math book. I gazed at the pages. These pages reminded me of my time. The same book and my school.

I delivered my lecture with full capability. One and a half hours later, I freed them. I collected my stuff, and like always, started watching my OTT stuff.

She came back to me.

'Let's go,' she said.

'Where to?' I asked.

'Somewhere, anywhere,' she said.

I was smiling.

'I knew you wanted this, but you didn't say,' she said.

'You understood already.'

'I heard about the unique Bharat Mata Mandir here,' I said further.

'What's the uniqueness of that temple?' She asked.

'I came to know that there is no statue of the particular god in it. The whole temple itself is a goddess and represents the entire country,' I said.

'Why do you constantly see things from a different angle? Although I have been to the temple, I have never viewed it that way,' she said.

'In what way?'

'The whole temple itself is a goddess and represents the entire country,' she teased me.

'Whatever it is, it is,' I said with a tinge of a smile.

We were on our Haridwar-Rishikesh National Highway, and as we crossed the Amrapur Ghat, suddenly she told me to take a right turn. Turning right, I found myself on a small, ungraded road that lay ahead of me.

'Where to?' I asked, in curiosity.

'Just speed up,' she said.

'They call it Lovers Point,' she briefed me.

Driving after almost one kilometre, we reached a calm and man-made small island in Haridwar, Lovers Point. This place in Haridwar is considered being one of the most exquisite locations. If you continue your journey a little further, you will reach the charming destination of Neelgaon, where the majestic river Ganga converges and forms a vast expanse of sand and stones, creating an enchanting beach-like ambiance. Contrary to our expectations, there was a noticeable absence of tourists in this location, with only a handful of individuals hailing from nearby regions. When standing in front, you can see the Chandighat bridge and if you look to the left, you'll be able to spot the Mansa Devi temple, while on the right side, the Chandi Devi temple will come into view. It seems that this bridge serves as a connection between both temples.

'I will call it a Peace Point, where you could sit alone for hours. Another beautiful place,' I said.

'What would you do if I told you to sit alone for hours?' I asked.

'I can't. I need something or someone.'

'Just look there,' she tapped on my hand.

We saw a girl and a boy kissing each other, hiding among the big concrete slabs.

'That's why they call it here, The Lovers Point,' I said.

She was blushing. It wasn't a normal thing for her.

'What if someone caught them?' I asked her.

'Police come here on a regular basis, but they would be done by then,' she said.

'Done by then!' I exclaimed.

'They will finish,' she said.

I laughed out loud. She blushed a little.

'Why are you laughing?'

'These concrete slabs should be made of cotton, then it would be more comfortable,' I said.

She wanted to speak, but she was hesitating. We were walking on the edge of the pedestrian path made by the concrete slabs. Besides these, a staircase-like structure was built to descend and enjoy the coolness of the Ganga water gathered there.

'Let's sit,' she said.

While we were seated, our legs were casually swaying, moving back and forth with no tension. Ducks could be seen drowning and then resurfacing from the water repeatedly. In that moment, my heart skipped a beat as I spotted a snake coiled up on top of a smooth stone. In an effort to warm up, it found solace by stretching out on the searing hot rocks. The Chandighat Bridge appeared as if a perfectly straight 3D line had been sketched in mid-air.

She was sitting silently.

'What if someone is observing us?' I said.

'So,' she said.

'What if someone is thinking about us like we were thinking about that couple?' I asked, picking on her.

'Is Mr. Writer afraid of the police?' She asked.

'Not in that way, but you're a minor,' I said.

'I know this place, the place where we are sitting, is publicly visible,' she said.

'Since when you're visiting this place?' I asked.

'Maybe three or four years,' she said.

'I had someone then,' she said.

'And…'

'And he died,' she said and stood up.

I shouldn't have asked.

'Let's head home, we will go to Bharat Mata temple some other day,' she said.

'Sorry,' I said.

She didn't respond.

I drove back and she, after dropping me, headed to hers.

'How come she has faced so much tragedy in her life?' I thought.

It was midnight, and my brother was cooking Maggi for us. I was cleaning the place. We were having a conversation regarding Maa and Papa. Mother and Father were in their fifties and so much obsessed with the village. They were simple souls, living their simple life, and had no particular need of something other than usual stuff.

My mother wakes up daily at 5 am, and at the very first, she cleans the house. My father plays some bhajans and goes for a walk to another village, which is 2 kms from our town.

Since I began observing, I have noticed a consistent routine in their lives. If they need to go somewhere, they always make an effort to return by evening. If not, they ensure to come back the following day, no matter what. By 10 am, she finishes her household chores and takes a moment to rest. Then, without fail, there is always some village gossip or discussions about the nearby village or relatives. Other neighbouring ladies often join in the conversation. Occasionally, they may argue and temporarily stop talking, but in the end, everything always works out. My mother cannot deviate from this routine. Despite any disagreements, they are ultimately happy and content.

Both of us were planning to go to the village. My brother started hating his job or any kind of job which imprisoned a person from 9 to 5.

'I want peace like our parents have,' he said.

He made a valid point. We left our homes in pursuit of wealth and success in our careers, but the price we pay is incredibly high. We sacrifice our time and the opportunity to create meaningful connections with families and our surroundings. Relocating to bustling metropolitan cities drastically changes our way of life. We find ourselves criticizing the simplicity of village life and its people. I grew up hearing stories about the ancient villages in our country from my grandfather. He used to describe a village as a close-knit community, where the arrival of a new child was celebrated by everyone. Children had the freedom to roam, sleep, and eat wherever they pleased. The villagers were known for their generosity, always eager to offer a helping hand.

Milk was a necessity for everyone, and it was readily available for anyone who desired a drink. We warmly welcomed guests with a variety of homemade dishes. The purity of our oil and ghee contributed to our strength. Many of our food items, such as dairy products, vegetables, and fruits, were almost free. Life was tranquil and uncomplicated. We cherished and protected nature, and in return, nature took care of us. I have fond memories of the village pond, surrounded by lush mango and guava trees.

When we travel outside our province for work, we miss out on the chance to age alongside our villagers, neighbours, and parents. We promised to come home regularly, but it never happens. City life consumes you. After a couple of years, we want to settle where we work. Thus, the village is lost, finally.

Thanks to our festivals, and the more significant thanks to the creator of our festivals that pulls people back to their homes.

We had our Maggie, and then we went to our rooms.

I saw the message. A simple dot was sent by her. I don't know whether she wants to tell or ask something.

I asked her, replying to her message.

Then she said, 'Nothing.'

I had been familiar with this 'nothing' for a significant period. I knew the very hard, intuitive meaning of this 'nothing.' This 'nothing' can contain a whole phase of life, which comprises either a few months or years, but for a teenager, I could assume for a dark secret or miserable tale that wouldn't matter after a couple of years.

'Just spit it out,' I said.

She took her time. A few minutes later, she replied.

'I miss him sometimes; he was the one when I got to know the bells of my heart could ring for someone. The first time I shivered was when he passed by. I miss my first…'

'I can understand. Keep him like a splendid memory. Don't be sad,' I replied.

'None of your closest friends have died or are dying, so you can't understand why I have every reason to be sad,' she explained her misery.

Indeed, she was right. No one can understand or feel the pain of the tragedies that didn't occur in one's life.

'Yeah, but I can relate to it. I have endured a different kind of arrow to my heart,' I said, tried to console her.

'How could a fifteen-year-old boy die? He shouldn't have died. Hadn't he died, I wouldn't be cursing this world,' she said.

'Unplanned happenings become the most terrible nightmares,' I said.

'I don't want to remember my teenage years as a pile of sorrows.'

'Just take a deep breath and sip some water.'

'Is that some kind of therapy too?'

No, it's just a diversion.

'Not therapy, but it helps.'

'Once I mentioned about reading books,' I added further.

'You want me to fail the exams?' She said.

'Can't you even spare half an hour for something useful?' I said.

'How could I read something which is irrelevant now?'

'The syllabus will help you pass the academics, but what you're dealing with needs some philosophical and psychological solution, some expert advice,' I said.

'I'm not forcing. I'm just suggesting,' I added.

'Okay, suggest some books.'

'We will discuss this tomorrow.'

'See you.'

Next day, she came alone. Her friend wasn't with her.

'What happened to your friend?' I asked, a bit worried.

'She won't come. Leave her,' she said.

'It will make my reputation bad,' I said.

'Is she that much important to you?' She asked, confused.

'As a tutor, it's my failure if I can't hold a student,' I clarified.

'Okay, I will bring her tomorrow,' she bluntly said.

'You told her not to come?' I asked.

'We just had a fight before coming here,' she said, her words crumbled. I understood that something happened.

'What happened?' I asked politely.

'Mother sent me to bring some herbs for my father, so I got a little late and she was waiting for me. I told her but she yelled at me and said she didn't want to come with me or use my scooty,' she said and sobbed.

'That's bad. She should've understood,' I said.

'She knew everything that is happening in my home, about my father. Still, no one cares,' she added further.

'Leave her, just dismiss her thoughts,' I said.

She remained silent.

'Want to go somewhere?' I asked a couple of minutes later.

'But we were supposed to study first.'

'Yes, we could, if you're mentally ready,' I said.

'No, let's go,' she said.

'Where could we go in such a morning?' I asked.

'Chilla would be the best,' she suggested.

Fifteen minutes later, we were on the Chilla Road. We were lost in our paces. The sun was yellow, like a ripe mango.

'You need to clear the clutter,' I broke the silence.

'Clear what the…' she replied normally.

'Should I stop somewhere or should I keep moving?' I interrupted.

'Keep moving,' she said.

'Clear the clutter means understanding what is urgent and what is important,' I said.

'I'm just a teenager,' she said.

'I expected this,' I said.

'You are talking to a stupid girl,' she said.

'You need to prioritize things. For me, it works,' I said.

'Actually, we will do a long discussion on it later. Just now, eat the breeze, smell the road, touch the light,' I said.

'I think my whole life would be like this, a mess,' she said.

'Nothing is permanent, dear,' I said.

'Don't say that.'

'What?'

'Dear.'

'Sorry, it just came out,' I said and felt disgusted.

'She must be thinking that I'm hitting on her.'

'Elders say dear, I don't want you to be a grandfather to me,' she said.

'Oh, okay.' I replied with a relief.

I parked the scooty over a bridge. Rishikesh was nearly 10 kms away. She didn't ask why I stopped. She stood beside me. I gazed at her. She was into something. Something was happening to me, too. The more I was going deeper into her life, the more liable she was becoming to me. Her mother believed in me, that's why she asked nothing of the boundaries.

'Clear the clutter won't work for you,' I said to her.

'Nothing will work for me. I'm a mess, I know,' she said.

'I don't know how to help you, Tanu, but truly, I want to.'

'I am aware that you want to.'

'My head just exploded when I tried to imagine myself in your position. Might be I can't feel what you're feeling exactly, but I'm with you as long as I can.'

'For two weeks?' She said in sarcasm.

'I will be talking to you by phone, or via text,' I said.

'Now you're talking shit,' she said.

'Just so you know — I'm not the guy who gets angry if you came late to pick me. I can wait. I can understand,' I said.

'I wish my so-called friends could say this to me,' she said.

'Why do you want them so desperately in your life?' I asked.

'Because I love them. They were different a couple of years ago. We had a bond, but after high school everything changed except for me. I am what I was a couple of years ago. I just miss the old version of them and they have become conditional,' she said.

'Just love them unconditionally. Maybe one day they will understand,' I said.

'But who will be patient enough to wait for the day when these stupid people start understanding me when I need these people today?' She said, angrily. Tears welled up in her eyes.

'We can't make them come to you. Maybe it's just time to accept the reality.'

'How does my home smell?' She asked a weird question.

'It smells good. I already appreciated it.'

'They said that my home smells like a medical store because of my father's medicines.'

'No one should say such things. They lack manners,' I said.

'Even if it's true, would you say it to someone whose father is struggling with cancer?' She said.

In that very moment, I was filled with empathy for her and longed for her to break free from it.

'Come, let's go,' I said.

'I don't want to go home.'

'Who's taking you home?'

I drove the scooty to Rishikesh. We passed the barrage and crossed the road linked to the AIIMS. A smile crept onto my face when I came across a momos stall and caught sight of its owner. I brought the scooty to a halt. His eyes resembled hers, both small and slanted.

'Let's have some momos.' I said to her, still smiling.

'I know why you are smiling. If my granny were here, she would have smiled too,' she said.

'So that's a regular thing in your family.'

We gobbled up those mouthwatering momos. Our taste sensibilities were heightened, leading us to purchase an additional plate.

'I heard there is a place like a beach in the Rishikesh.' I said, licking my fingers.

'Yeah, that place is photogenic. We should've brought a camera.'

'Smartphone won't work?'

'I prefer DSLR. Smartphone cameras are just for fun, not for actual photography.'

'Look at this photo.' She said and showed me a portrait picture of her with her mother.

'That's exquisite.'

'Even if you buy the costliest smartphone, it won't capture like it.'

'You love photography...don't you?' I asked her.

'Yes, I want to take millions of pictures of myself and anything that I find attractive.'

'That sounds beautiful.'

'Do you have a camera?' I asked.

'No, it's expensive stuff. I usually take it on rent.'

We parked the scooter at the Laxman Jhoola, drove over the stunning metal-rope hanging bridge, and arrived at the beach. One could argue that the location resembled a beach because of the wide river and the presence of large stones and sand on the shore. It was also an excellent photo opportunity. The backdrop of the river, with the stone as its centrepiece, offers an incredible photo opportunity. I captured an image of her.

'Next time, we will come with a DSLR,' she said.

'I would love to,' I said, and we drove back home.

'We will enjoy dosa in the evening,' she said before departing.

'I would love to,' I said.

I waited for her call in the evening. She didn't text or call. I was watching a movie. The movie took almost three hours, and in the meantime, I forgot to check my phone. I checked it, but still there was no call or text.

'Everything's alright?' I texted her.

She didn't reply. My brother had come, so I made myself busy with other chores. Before going to bed, I checked my phone once more. There was no reply. I felt a bit tense.

'Maybe she is with her father.' I thought.

Next day I waited for her to come. She didn't appear. I was in a loophole because I was wondering why her disappearance was bothering me so much. She wasn't texting. Her DP was the same.

'My father is hospitalized,' she texted back in the afternoon.

'Should I come if that makes you feel better?' I asked her.

'No, I will come to you,' she said.

She came in the evening, and at the very first I took her to the dosa stall. I wanted her to get out of this miserable maze.

'How's your father now?' I asked.

'He can't metabolize liquid; her stomach gets filled with water,' she said.

'That's disturbing,' I said.

'Think how we deal with him; he is like a child now. He insists on the things that would make him worse. Doctors drain the excess water through tubes by drilling in his stomach,' she said.

'I wish for some miracle to cure him, to grant him a pain-free life,' I said.

'Now is the perfect moment for miracles to occur if any exist in the world. I want him to live for my mother and brother at least,' she said.

'I wish,' I said.

The dosa maker was a South Indian guy. He was not over 18, and his Hindi accent was funny. He had an assistant, and he used to abuse him in inaccurate Hindi, which made him actually funnier.

'Why did you refuse me to come to the hospital?' I asked.

'I don't want anyone to come to the hospital. You could visit him at home,' she said.

'I just don't want anyone to see him aching, crying in pain,' she said further.

'From a little girl. How fast is she growing? Her funny and school girl life was going to end.' I thought.

'Should we go to temples this time?' I asked her.

'Why temples?'

'You should also give it a try, ask something from the divine and perhaps a miracle will occur.'

'You're saying this? A writer who is far from this fake world. I didn't expect this from you at least. Don't be like them.'

'Then go for just a casual visit. We will go to Mansa Devi.'

'Three ways to go to Mansa Devi. A ropeway, a stairway and a trek of three kilometres.'

'How many times have you gone there?'

'I don't know, many times.'

'We will trek.'

'Okay then, 10 am tomorrow.'

'After studies, you have practiced nothing for two days.'

'Okay, let's go home.' She said, and we drove home.

Chapter-6

Beyond the Boundaries

She came early, and I was ready too. I shared some math tricks with her and passed on some advice I had learned from my teacher. We had an incredible math session that lasted for an hour and a half.

After she answered the questions I had given her, we made our way to the Mansa Devi shrine. Opting to trek, we crossed the Laltharaav Bridge and turned left. I drove the scooter past the parked cars as we followed the road parallel to the mountain. Driving through the gate, we eventually reached another gate where we had to park. Bringing the scooty to a stop, I noticed a place, and she invited me to join her. It turned out that we had a stunning panoramic view of Har Ki Pauri. The sight was truly breathtaking. I made sure to capture the vibrant saffron colours of the temples and the presence of the surveillance tower in my pictures. From that spot, I could also observe the diversion of the Ganga Canal, which clarified the Haridwar mental map for me. I couldn't resist taking a picture of the beautiful vista.

We were hiking. For a rest, people were seated sideways, and some restrooms were in the middle. There was verbal fighting and abuse between the two beggars. Some sellers were sitting sideways and selling the pious fruits and stuff...*The Ramphal* and a rock substance *The Shilajeet*, which is widely used as an immunity and testosterone booster and for males, it is considered being the best natural Viagra and highly used in metaphors for hyperactive persons in India.

We arrived at this magnificent temple entryway.

Upon arriving at the temple, I was awestruck by the grandeur of the complex, which boasts intricate and striking architecture. It is worth noting that this structure has a storied past, with origins dating back centuries ago.

Manasa or Mansa, a form of Shakti, is worshipped in the temple. It is said that the temples created from the mind of Kashyapa, the Rishi. Mansa is known as the sister of Vasuki the Naga. The name Mansa means wish, and it is believed that the goddess will grant the desires of true believers. To have their wishes fulfilled, people tie threads to the tree in the temple. Once their wishes are granted, they return to the temple to remove the thread from the tree. Offerings such as coconuts, fruits, garlands, and incense sticks are presented to appease Mansa. The temple holds great religious significance and is dedicated to the Hindu goddess Mansa Devi, who is worshipped worldwide. Praying to this deity is believed to bring good luck and blessings, making it a popular pilgrimage site for devoted individuals. The Mansa Devi Temple is considered a Siddh Peeth, a significant place of attainment. Those who worship at Siddh Peeths are said to have their desires fulfilled. Haridwar is home to three

Peeths, including the Chandi Devi Temple and Maya Devi Temple. Within the shrine, there are two deities — one with eight arms and the other with three heads and five arms.

We were sitting on a giant rock where people have written their names by carving.

'What's the greatest disappointment you find in today's generation?' She asked.

'You mean the generation of the 21st century?' I asked.

'Yes, those who were born after 2000 or Gen Z?'

I chuckled a bit.

I have grown to know this chuckling of yours.

'What?'

'You always chuckle before saying something which proves our generation stupid.'

'That's not true. If that were true, I wouldn't have told you anything,' I defended myself.

'Then tell me because now it feels like I should've been born in the 90s.'

'The world has changed in every decade whether we come from 70s, 80s, or 90s, but still during that time the life was at a slow pace. We were cultural and had morals, but do you know why the elder ones are surprised to see today's generations?'

'Because we are too fast,' she said.

'The reasons are the technologies, the food and the transportation. I'm not against any of it, but most of this generation uses these in every bad way possible. Technology comes to ease our work and to save time. Instagram and Facebook are two great platforms to promote your work and build brands, but how do you and your friends use it? Just for a few likes and reels to kill the time. Your eyes get affected and, in the end, your brain is unhappy because you have wasted so much time. The productivity is zero. With just a click on your mobile device, you can access most things. We don't go outside just because of this tool. The second thing is the food — especially the fast food. The two-minute noodles and the Chinese stuff. You feel hungry — just go to the nearest shop, grab a processed ketchup and noodles, and the meal is ready in two minutes. Every processed food is a poison. It imbalances our hormones and affects our health. And the third is transportation — now everyone has a vehicle. We don't walk because we are always in a hurry. These three things have changed everything, and they have come into existence in the 21st century — we forgot to wait. In the older era, food was organic, the pace was slow. Patience was there. I'm actually worried about what will happen after fifty years.'

'Aren't these supposed to be wonderful inventions?'

'These are good, but most of the people aren't taking these as we should. A single message from a friend can break your heart. Look how vulnerable we have become. We end relationships via texts today — even without proper closure. This is dangerous. Most teenagers are destroying themselves because of the complete dependence on these devices.'

'How do you utilize your free time?' She asked.

'Not on reels, either a good movie or series, a book maybe, and if not anything, either I sleep or walk.' I said.

'I will delete my Instagram account, even WhatsApp too,' she said with a slight enthusiasm.

'Can you live without it?' I asked.

'I will. These reels kill my time.'

I wanted to tell her not to delete the account, just use it wisely, but since she had committed, I wanted to see whether she was capable of it.

'It's your choice,' I said.

'Let's go,' she said.

Finally, we landed back. She went back to her home.

During the night, I WhatsApp messaged her to come at 10 am the next day, but as I saw her profile, she had deleted the account.

'What!' I exclaimed.

I texted her: Tomorrow's timing is 10 am.

'Okay,' she replied, and nothing else. There is one thing revolving inside my mind — what if she didn't want to delete the accounts and she did it because of my sake?

'Let's find out tomorrow,' I thought.

She came at the right time. Today's plan was only for studying. She did her work as I suggested. We didn't talk about deleting accounts. I hoped she would tell me anything about this action of hers, but she didn't. She was silent. I was observing the circle she was drawing in her notebook. She wrote fast. She wanted to finish the work as soon as possible and wasn't speaking. Somehow, it disturbed my peace.

She stopped her writing and gently rubbed the pen with her thumb — like I used to do in the exam when I thought deeply about the answer.

'My cousin is coming tomorrow, and we have planned to go to Chandi Devi this Sunday,' she finally broke the silence.

'That will be good. More people, more fun,' I said.

'I wanted him to meet you,' she said.

'Sure, why not?'

'You shouldn't have deleted WhatsApp,' I said further—it just came out of my mouth.

'You won't believe but yesterday was very peaceful — no notifications and no time to waste. I felt good,' she said.

I wanted to tell her that we just have to control the way we use our phone and at least she should install WhatsApp. Instagram is her choice.

'Okay.'

'How old is your cousin?' I asked.

'Same as me,' she said.

'Can you arrange a DSLR?' She asked.

'I will — for sure,' I said.

Next day, I arranged a DSLR, Canon 200D Mark II. I called her. I never operated a camera, but she knew everything about it. She took it from me and instructed me how to operate it and she was very good at it. Later, she instructed me about the lenses, the autofocus, manual mode, and many other things.

'Where did you learn all this?' I asked her.

'One of my classmates owns a DSLR,' she replied.

'Hmm, so when will we begin?' I asked.

'Tomorrow morning, I will call you.'

As the next day's sun appeared, I woke up and got ready and within fifteen minutes, we were at the entrance. Her cousin greeted me — I almost forgot that I was the senior- most there. After a long phase in my life, I was feeling like I was 18 years old. She was carrying the camera. There was a huge bell at the entrance — we rang it many times. Our journey started.

Another group of five people was ahead of us and they continuously chanted *'Jor se Bolo Jai Mata Di.'* Such an exceptional energy and full of the holy vibe it was. Two people were old in their group, but as I have said earlier — the power of faith. They were clapping and going.

We began our ascent to the Chandi Devi temple, which was perched atop the Neel Parvati Hill.

As we trek up the winding path, we were rewarded with breathtaking vistas of the surrounding hills and valleys. The flora and fauna on this trail were diverse and captivating, with each step bringing you closer to the marvels of nature. The journey was arduous, but the views made it all worth it. Almost twenty minutes later, she made us stop for photography. She handed me the camera.

'Use the bigger lens,' she said.

I have learnt that a bigger lens was used for portrait photography. So, I put on the bigger lens and clicked her pics. She told me to signal with my thumb when I clicked the photo so that she could change her posture. And that enigmatic girl let her secret come to light. I've only had official and informal encounters with her. Normally, she would wear casual clothing, but today was different. She had loose hair that fluttered in the breeze. She stood out there because of her black sports shoes, black trousers, and black jacket. I clicked almost fifty photos, but when a girl prepares herself for photography — she is hardly satisfied.

'We will click the rest on the top,' she said.

The trail was dotted with several rest stops, where you can catch your breath and soak in the scenic beauty of the landscape. We halted to catch our breaths. Her face had turned red. Her cousin was a funny boy, and he was mocking her as she got tired far sooner than us. The last stretch of the trek involved climbing a flight of stairs that lead to the Chandi Devi temple. The temple is a beautiful edifice that exudes a sense of serenity and divinity. It is said that the temple was built in the 8th century by Adi Shankaracharya.

The temple is dedicated to the Hindu goddess Chandi, who is believed to symbolize power and strength. Devotees from all over the world who come to seek her blessings worship the goddess. The temple's location is one reason it is considered a must-visit destination in Haridwar.

Our trekking time to get there was sixty minutes. The store owners were contacting us to offer our shoes for free placement. However, I was aware that nothing in this world is free. In order to ensure the protection of our shoes, we had to compensate them for making offerings to the goddess.

The inner sanctum of the temple houses a statue of Chandi Devi adorned with ornaments and flowers. The temple also has smaller shrines dedicated to other Hindu deities, such as Lord Ganesh, Lord Shiva, and Lord Hanuman. I don't align myself with any religious beliefs or atheism. I can't just ignore the faith of millions of people, so we purchased the offering, which contained flowers, incense sticks, coconut, chunri. We were in a queue and, as purohit said; we did everything, including lighting a diya.

The Chandi Devi Temple is more than just a place of pilgrimage; it is also a centre for those seeking spiritual enlightenment. The serene atmosphere of the temple, combined with its spiritual energy, can have a calming effect on the mind and cultivate inner tranquillity.

After leaving the temple, we proceeded towards another temple located on a different hill. We enjoyed a meal at a restaurant and eagerly ate the aloo poodi. Monkeys were plentiful. People were offering them snacks, and they were among us frequently.

Then we came to a corner point of a hill, which is said to be the suicide point. As I stood up at the end of the hill, it was scary because deep down there was a dreadful valley. A tree had grown out of the steep cliff, and someone carved a name on the trunk of the tree. It was scary because whoever did this — he had to climb up to that trunk and that was almost suicide. The Chandighat bridge was visible from here. The vehicles seemed to be tiny toys.

She called her cousin to click a picture of us. It was a sour-sweet gesture from her.

'For memories,' she said.

Then I took that camera and shot a tonne of photos of her and her cousin. There was a concrete slab — especially placed there for sitting purpose. While we were sitting on that slab, her cousin was capturing the scenery.

'You're looking pretty,' I finally complimented her.

I noticed she glanced at me, as if she was longing to hear these words from me. A gaze filled with intensity. I assumed something was blossoming inside both of us for the both of us. I felt my heart being pulled towards her. Her intense gaze had me under her spell for a while. Brushing back her hair from her forehead as the wind blew across it, she said, 'My cousin said that I was looking cute this morning.'

'Well, you are,' I said.

'But I'm troubled.'

'That makes you more of it.'

'I feel less troubled today.'

'Have you prayed for your father?'

'Yes, His health is adversely affecting. He is frustrated and my mother becomes more agitated because he wants to accomplish so much but cannot.'

'Should I visit your home, if you say so?'

'But you won't be entertained there.'

'I don't want to. I want to meet your father.'

'I always ask God to ease his pain. I can't stand him when he cries.'

'Your cousin seems to be more curious about our conversation.'

She looked at him. He was pretending to click the photos. She laughed.

'He takes keen interest in other's gossip, especially mine.'

'I think we should go now. Sun's up.'

It took us hardly 30 minutes to come down. We went directly to her home, where her mother and grandmother were preparing lunch.

I greeted her grandmother.

'How's he holding up?' I asked.

'In deep sleep now, as long as he sleeps, we could breathe. Otherwise…,' her voice crumbled before she could finish.

'We prayed for him.'

'I hope God hears your prayer.'

'Can I see him?' I asked her mother.

Her mother took me to his room. He was so skinny. It felt like I was staring at a body preserved in a scientific lab for a long time because of the discoloured skin. The veins and bones of the hands were clearly visible. The shoulders were also completely missing — the skin was just serving to cover the skeleton. On seeing him, suddenly it came out of my mind, *'O God, give him freedom from this unbearable pain'.*

'Tanu, go and bring these things.'

Her mother sends her to buy some stuff.

I went to her room and sat in the same place.

'How is she doing?' She asked me.

'She is working hard,' I said.

'Frequently, I feel like I don't even know myself, and I become really upset with my kids, especially Tanu. I don't even have time to explain about it later. You can understand very well how much my children have to endure at such an age. If possible, explain it to Tanu from my side. She gets offended and stops talking. People claim to be with you, but there is a big difference between that promise and actually being there,' she said.

'To be honest, she is extremely intelligent and will mature at a faster rate. She understands you as well as her father's sufferings. She needs time,' I said.

'I hope she is in excellent hands.'

'Of course, just call me whenever you need to ask anything,' I convinced her.

'The car which is parked below belongs to you?' I asked.

'Yes, that's our car, but no one's driving. Sometimes her uncle uses it.'

'You want to go somewhere?' She asked.

'No, no, I was just curious, nothing else,' I said.

'You can drive it if you need to...do you drive?'

'Yes, but I haven't driven in years.'

Tanu came in with tea and samosas. We devoured our snacks, and for a few minutes; we were blissful. I distracted them from the misery for a few minutes. Her mother was talking about my family and the brother.

I asked Tanu to drop me.

'No one comes to us now; I've seen my mother smile after a long time. You should come here regularly,' she said to me.

'I will, as much as needed. Can you drive the car?' I asked her.

'I'm a teenager. How could I?' she said.

'Next month you will be an adult,' I said.

'How do you know?'

'I just...know.'

'How? Please tell.'

'On our next trip.'

'You irritate me a lot.'

'It's a part of my syllabus,' I chuckled.

'Okay, where will we go?'

'Wherever you want.'

'Okay, tomorrow then. Bye.' She dropped me off and left.

Chapter-7

Suffer by Choice

The following day, she arrived at the same time to meet me. I had my laptop resting on my lap while I sat cross-legged, dressed in a vest.

As soon as I heard her scooty, I quickly changed my clothes.

'My exams are coming; it is only a week away,' she said, nervously.

'Keep on preparing at your normal pace,' I said.

'This time I'm afraid of falling.'

'If you think beforehand, then definitely you will. We won't go anywhere today if you have such a scary feeling.'

'No, since I'm scared, so today is the perfect day to visit Third Siddhpeeth, Maya Devi Temple.'

That made me smile.

Without delay, we picked up the scooty and set out for our next mission amidst the scorching winds in this winter season. The Maya Devi temple was on the same route I had taken to Har Ki Pedi. There were fewer people, so it wasn't as crowded. The steam was coming out of Ganga ji. Some people were still taking a dip in it. The sky was lightly foggy, with a white blanket covering it, and everyone eagerly awaited the appearance of the Sun. A large number of bonfires were kindled at the edge of the road.

Within 15 minutes, we reached there.

According to legend, the temple is believed to be located where the heart and navel of the goddess Sati fell, thus making it a Shakti Peetha. The Adhisthatri deity of Haridwar is Goddess Maya. She is a divine being with three heads and four arms, believed to be a manifestation of Shakti. Mayapuri was the previous name given to Haridwar in reverence to this deity. The temple is regarded as a Siddha Peetha, a sacred site where people believe their desires come true.

The construction of the temple took place during the eleventh century. Out of the ancient temples in Haridwar, only three have managed to remain intact throughout time. This temple, along with Narayana-shila and Bhairava Temple, is one of them. Inside the inner shrine, you will find statues of goddesses, Maya, with Kali on the left and Kamakhya on the right. Shakti lives in the inner shrine, along with two other goddesses believed to be her forms. To reach the temple, simply head east of Har Ki Pauri. It is easily accessible by both buses and auto-rickshaws. When visiting Haridwar, devout followers often consider it an essential destination.

After offering our prayers and dwelling in our wishful thoughts, we returned.

I have started to feel blissful with her — a current rose in my arteries as soon as I realized that she was about to come.

'Let's go eat biryani today?' I asked curiously.

'No, let's go to another nice place,' she replied. Her answer made me feel like she was in a hurry.

'We can go to the remaining places after your exams, but don't be in such a hurry.'

'That's not true—I actually really enjoy the place we're heading to at the moment, and I've been going there since I was a child.'

'Let's go then.'

Once again, we embarked on our red scooty and headed towards another destination. As she was giving me instructions, I followed along and we eventually arrived at a new location in Kankhal. Our journey took us through the vibrant market of Kankhal before we finally arrived at the Daksha Prajapati temple, where we safely parked our scooty.

That temple was exquisite.

'I know about this temple, but I wanted to come here on my next visit,' I said.

'You don't plan for the temples, the temple invites you, you're his plan,' she said.

According to the Shiv Purana, the origin of the temple is based on a mythological tale. According to the story, Brahma's prayer was answered, and Sati was born as Jagdamba or Bhagwati, the most powerful Shakti among the Hindu gods. She was born in Kankhal as the daughter of Daksh Prajapati. Legend has it that Sati performed intense worship to win Lord Shiva's hand in marriage. Eventually, Lord Shiva agreed to marry her. However, tensions arose between King Daksh and his son-in-law. According to a story in the Shiv Purana, King Daksh organized a grand Yajna in Kankhal and invited everyone — gods, rishis, and munis — but purposely ignored his son-in-law. When Sati learned about the event, she convinced Lord Shiva to let her attend. During the event, her father insulted Lord Shiva, which enraged Sati. She was so furious that she jumped into the flames. Upon hearing the tragic news, Lord Shiva sent Veerbhadra, one of his strongest warriors, to Kankhal. Veerbhadra beheaded King Daksh and cremated him in the Yajna fire. At the request of Lord Vishnu and the other gods, Lord Shiva manifested as the self-formed linga. Although King Daksh was dead, Lord Shiva resurrected him with the head of a goat to complete the Yajna. Daksh deeply regretted his actions. Lord Shiva declared that every year during the month of Sawan, which is very dear to him, Kankhal would be his abode. Devastated by the loss of his beloved consort, Lord Shiva roamed across the universe carrying her lifeless body.

According to myths, it is believed that Lord Vishnu used his Sudarshan Chakra to separate Sati's body parts from Lord Shiva, thus relieving him of his immense sorrow. The places where these severed body parts fell are now revered as Shaktipeeths. To commemorate this significant event, temples were constructed at these locations in Kankhal.

The main Daksheshwar Temple, along with other temples, is located by a serene tributary of the Ganga River at the foothills of the Shivalik Ranges. It includes the Hanuman Temple and Das Mahavidya Temple. Divided into two sections, the Temple features a Yajna Kund and a Shiv Linga, both of which devotees worship by offering water. The temple walls vividly depict the entire story of King Daksh's yajna and its consequences. The temple grounds revolve around a sacred banyan tree, believed to be thousands of years old, which captures everyone's attention. Throughout the year, the temple attracts devotees from all over the country and abroad. During the month of Sawan, there is a significant influx of Lord Shiva devotees. The occasion of Shivratri also draws a large number of devotees who come here seeking Lord Shiva's blessings.

We were sitting under the banyan tree, on the stairs that lead to the Ganga ji. Some people were taking baths, and some were pouring the droplets of the Jal over their bodies.

'I heard the story of this temple and King Daksha,' I said.

'It's fascinating.'

'How is it fascinating?' She asked.

'It's a story full of extreme emotions — love, anger, mourn and grief,' I said.

'Despite being a God, even Shiva felt the wrath of death. He felt disgusted after being insulted. He grieved after the death of his spouse and mourned in the memory of his love,' she said.

'How will my mother feel when my father's gone?' she added.

'Don't say that, never ever repeat this. We always expect life before death. Wish him a speedy recovery.'

'Can't you see the truth even after seeing him lying in the bed like an undead corpse?'

'Still, I wish for a miracle, for the sake of your family.'

'Our family won't survive if he continues in this state. He is affecting everyone.'

'What do you want?'

'I want God to end his suffering. Our lives are at hold. We are in the middle of nowhere. They were talking about the transplant, but can his body accept the new liver?'

'At least they are optimistic, even in the hospital's doctors take every chance, even if it's little.'

'Everyone knows he is going to die, even his own mother, and if my mother becomes careless for just one day, he won't survive. It's she who is fighting with death for him. My mother knows that the transplant will cost us everything and there is less than 1% chance that he could survive the operation, but she wants to go against all the odds.'

'She is a supreme lady and doing exactly what a wife should do to her husband. Death is a matter of chance; you are foreseeing his death because of his health status, but you can't even predict your next moment. Remember — we expect life before death. Don't expect death because it is certain. It will come to everyone one day, eventually,' I said.

'You should spend time with your father, seek his blessings,' I said further.

She said nothing. As I watched, her eyes became wet. I wanted to console her by letting her head rest on my shoulder.

I just mumbled. 'Everything will be fine.'

'I would've gone mad if you hadn't come into my life.'

'It's just destiny. Soon you'll understand things as they are.'

She nodded her head.

'I will come to you on alternate days for queries,' she said.

'As you wish, just prepare well and I think you should install WhatsApp. You can send me the questions,' I said.

'Okay, I will.'

She left me at my place, and I saw her scooty vanishing into the crowd. The seed of blossom and care had sprouted inside my heart for her. Whatever mess she was — she was honest. Desperate for love and care, affected by the traumatic ambience, and learning to survive through all of this. I was so much invested in her I have forgotten myself to some extent.

The saying seemed to be true:

'Provide a man love, food, and home, and he will forget his purpose.'

I may be simple and a man who couldn't do harm to anyone, but I was financially broke. Despite being a postgraduate, I didn't have a single penny in my account, and I never cared to deposit something in it because of the penalty charges. My brother didn't know it, but I had an unclosed personal loan and my email was full of notices of unpaid EMIs from the last six months. I was about to declare NPA, a non-performing asset and they were going to block my CIBIL.

My brother provided me with the basic expenses, and sometimes my father. They said nothing to me regarding my unemployment, but in their heart, there was a sickness for me and I knew it. 'You literally have to understand the value of money one day,' my father had said it.

I took on three different jobs with various roles, but I left each of them before completing a year. The fault wasn't in the jobs— people were doing them—but with me. None of my bosses were happy with me. I was late for work, and the work was casual. They had to redo my work because of my unproductivity. I remember when I resigned from my third job; the boss was happy. He was not happy because I resigned. Instead, he was happy because he assumed I had finally found something to do. He was an expressionless man. I barely saw him smile. Just work-oriented, totally and insanely.

'I know you didn't belong here, and sometimes I felt like you too, but it's too late for me. I have three daughters. But you must take your chances. Whatever it is, you take it. A very few men in this world have the privilege to live for themselves, to suffer by choice,' he said.

'Thanks Sir,' I said.

'Keep suggesting the books, TV series, and movies to the people. It's the best skill I have seen in you so far. I have seen some of your suggested movies, and they were just jaw- dropping,' he said.

'And he who lives his life on his own choices suffers extensively, so, I wish you to get whatever you seek. I wish you all the best.'

That was one of the beautiful phrases I had heard. I concluded that I had to suffer. And for the past few days, I didn't feel like suffering but enjoying it. She did something inside me.

I was lying in the bed, deep lost in thought, and suddenly the gate was brutally opened, like someone was draining anger over it.

It was my brother with two of his friends — drunk. They had beer in their hands.

'I…will…kill…that…bastard…HR…' My brother was drunk and angry.

I went to his room. He saw and ignored me. One of his friends offered me a beer can, but I refused.

'What happened?' I asked him.

'He did not get his increment.'

I turned back and returned to my room.

'He won't understand my pain. Don't tell him,' my brother was saying this to one of his friends.

When they were leaving, they left a beer in the kitchen.

I had a sudden realization, which led me to grab a beer and finish it in a single swig.

He was watching me.

'Now he will understand,' he said.

'Sit here,' he added.

'The whole family is disturbed because of you. Father is going to retire in a couple of years. You have practiced two particular habits throughout all these years — 'ignorance' and 'carelessness'. No matter whoever says whatever to you, if the topic isn't in your interest, you wouldn't even argue; you just…ignore. Just tell me one thing, my brother —how would your ignorance and carelessness feed you in the future?' He asked, but I kept quiet. I wanted to hear him out.

'Can't your books or mobile screen tell you to earn a coin? If I leave this job right now, you can't even pay the room rent. You can't pay four thousand rupees a month for this room. Isn't it a shame that your value isn't even equal to the room rent? You're the elder one. Have you ever seen a younger one taking care of his elder one? You're a shameless elder brother,' he taunted me brutally.

I didn't argue with him because he was right. Rightly so, he was a truly concerning brother of mine. He fed me, gave me my own room to respect my privacy, and wouldn't have teased me if he enjoyed his job. Something unfortunate occurred to him because of his frustration. I couldn't help but stare at his perspiring face. He finished his beer.

'Despite being the most educated individual in our family, this is what you have achieved. Your brain is deteriorating. If your education doesn't result in financial gain, it's similar to a book that's been buried in the desert.'

'I want to be a writer.'

'People write when they age, when they gather experience, and most importantly, when their account balance is in six, seven, or eight figures. You're just digging a grave for your career. You wrote a book already. How many readers did you get? Five or ten? One copy of your book is supporting the fourth foot of my shelf,' he said.

I looked at the shelf.

'You won't get it, ever.' I said and stood up. I removed my book from under the shelf and wiped the dust.

'Okay, just tell me, when will you find your tree?' He asked.

'Tree?'

'A tree is necessary for Buddha. That's where he got his wisdom. Or are you waiting for the full moon?'

'Buddha won't be a Buddha if he had a brother like you,' I said and moved to my room where she was sitting.

I almost paused. I realized the gate was open, and she came discreetly.

'Give me that,' she asked for the book.

'I would read it someday and don't worry, I won't use it to support the foot of my shelf,' she said.

'You were eavesdropping,' I said.

'Sorry for that. I just don't want to disturb the atmosphere. It was a rare sight,' she said.

I chuckled.

'How much were you earning in your last job?'

'Around 40k,' I said.

'And how much is your brother earning right now?'

'25k, you should not conclude anything,' I said to her,

'The life I chose is hard and my brother reminds me of it from time to time. He will be fine by tomorrow,' I said.

'If you continued your job till now, then you could've a decent saving for your next assignment,' she said.

'There would be no assignment if I continued my job. I would be a different man with a partially enabled brain just to please his boss. In any corporation, a man's only job is to please his boss. If you want to be your own boss and labour for your own work, then it has a price and I'm paying for it,' I said.

'So, what's these degrees for? You should be an engineer by degree,' she asked.

'Degrees can't be meaningless, ever. When I was pursuing these, each assignment and project has contributed to me whatever I am today. When you solve a problem, prepare for semester exams or competitive exams, your brain's ability to handle problems improves. The more able your brain is, the more you will tackle the obstacles and it will expand the universe of reasoning for you. Degrees are achievements, but we just take them as a criterion for a job. I'm an engineer and I always will be, but the field in which I engineer something will be of my choosing,' I said.

'And you would engineer something in literature,' she said.

'I want to.'

'What if you don't succeed? What if people just hate your version of the world?'

'I will improvise and I will die improvising.'

'How could you read these books?' She pointed towards a stack of my collection.

'Okay, how could you figure out which movie you want to see?'

'Whichever is popular or has my favourite stars in it.'

'Same here. I read popular books, award-winning books, and controversial books. You pick a book and just read ten pages of it, then the book will decide automatically whether or not it will turn more pages for you. Book reading is boring if you aren't excited about what's inside.'

'Books don't have visuals; movies have visuals.'

'If I say "She stood tall and confident, her white skin glowing in the sunlight. Her chubby cheeks and wide forehead gave her a youthful appearance, but her chinky eyes betrayed a sharp intelligence and a fierce determination. She was not someone to be trifled with." Didn't you sketch it inside your brain?'

'Yes.'

'Whose?'

'I know, just go ahead. It sounded so nice,' she said, and I smiled.

'All I want to say is that books are the first virtual realities; you can create your type of visuals, not the same that you see on the screen. Books explore a virtual cinema inside you. Reading makes you smart because now your brain is more able,' I said.

'Distraction pulls me away. Why can't I focus for a few hours on my studies or learning? I came here to study. I couldn't do it inside my home,' she said.

'Just do what you want to...quietly,' I said.

She was completely into her preparation. I didn't disturb her. In the other room, my brother was snoring. And I was sitting in the corner chair, pretending to read a novel, but each second was passing hollow. My brother's words were hammering in my head. My own theory of existence was driving me crazy, but my brother was right. How would I survive without money?

I came here for two or three weeks, but I didn't know how much time had passed.

'At least I should earn for my pocket money.' I thought.

'Can't your friends come here? I can teach the whole batch,' I asked her.

At first, she felt odd because I knew she didn't want anyone sitting beside her. She wanted only 'her' time with me, but she understood I needed money.

'It's a good idea, I can support you in that. I can get you at least ten students,' she said to me.

'That would be fine.'

'But you need to teach them something else, other than PCM.'

'Right now, they need a computer science tutor.'

'I can teach them programming languages.'

'Okay, I will bring them. Now you can pay the room rent easily.'

I gazed at her face. For a couple of seconds, I felt like she was insulting me. I didn't want her to take me as a broke and poor guy. I wanted her to understand that I could do a job that paid at least 50k, but my intentions were to be my own boss.

'No, I won't teach. I thought something productive to earn money,' I said and dropped her idea.

'She won't tell me how I should earn. I have to make a living by myself.' I thought.

'Okay, but how come you're broke...I mean...weren't you supposed to be smart enough to have at least some savings for yourself?' She asked.

'Has anyone in your school taught you about finance management or financial education?'

'No, but isn't it obvious that we should have money?'

'We must have money; I believe money is something that can do miracles after God.'

'...and I had my savings but the things I'm seeking right now took a lot more time than I expected and everything is collapsing, but I'm a low maintenance guy. My monthly expenses will be far less than yours.'

'I can see that. You barely have over four t-shirts. You wore nothing new, and I can easily predict what you would wear next,' she said and smiled. I smiled too.

'You were saying something about financial education?' she asked.

'We are taught to have enough money to live a decent life. Get a job and earn. Get promoted and earn more. Money isn't the only thing that should be used just to pay bills and purchasing the needy stuff. Money is more than what it seems, and it directly affects the way of doing things. It amplifies your character. Your brain works differently when money is in your possession. As I have said, it can do miracles. Even in a traffic jam, a person sitting in a Rolls Royce or in another luxury car can work on his idea. He could just mute the world. He can attend an online meeting or could make his next presentation because money has brought him a miraculous vehicle that could provide him with every comfort so that he can use every second of time while travelling. We weren't taught in school how to manage our finances and how the flow of money occurs in our system. No one ever taught the students about savings, investing, and methods to make more money. I have read some books, and now I know how much money, opportunities, and time, I have wasted in my past. Had someone provided me some knowledge about the importance of money or guided me about investing and startups earlier, then maybe today I would've owned a publishing house.'

'You want to own a publishing house?' She asked.

'Apart from a writer, yes. Someday, I hope to sit in an office in my own publication house. I want to publish my stories and articles. I want to hire some aspiring writers and authors,' I said.

'You have big goals.'

'But achievable,' I said.

'I can only wish you the best for your dreams.'

'You're the first one to acknowledge and validate my dreams, and someone who wished me the best.'

'Maybe you didn't explain to others like you explained to me.'

'A working professional won't appreciate these because that will be something beyond the boundaries for him. A businessman or an entrepreneur can understand this.'

'But I'm neither of them.'

'You are new and uncorrupted by the system.'

'You have always so much to tell,' she said.

'If you want to sort your life out. Start writing a diary.'

'No, I can't write. Writing is boring, especially the diary.'

'If you want your brain to function more, then you should write. I recommend writing to every person on this planet. Writing pushes your brain; it makes you think. You can't write without thinking.'

'Earlier, you said that we must read, and now you're saying we must write.'

'That's the point. You can't write better if you don't read, like you can't be an excellent speaker if you're not a good listener.'

'Work, jobs are essential for living, isn't it? But art is something that we live for. People take vacations in a year just for art. Every beautiful thing that makes you say "wow" is an art. Novels, songs, paintings, engineering, and even natural sights are unique pieces of art. Artists are the lords of this world. They save people from getting mad.' I elaborated.

'Now I feel, why am I even preparing for the exams?'

'It's necessary, for the noble pursuits and the sake of survival.'

'I want to see myself for what I live for in the future.'

I was stuck in two parallel worlds. One world was with her and one was without her. She had begun to know me and my emptiness. She knew my frustration a bit, even so, she had a hope from me…a little at least. Her heart wasn't corrupted. For her, I was a decent human. She wasn't judging me by any kind of status.

Or she was aware that although I'm trapped right now, I'm still capable of a lot. Whatever that was, every time I saw my brother's face, I was reminded of reality. Subsequently, I discovered that I also had some obligations. My parents were approaching their fifties. I needed to be a responsible brother and son.

However, if you read a few phrases about the world's greatest individuals, you'll see that none of them had any familial obligations. They disregarded everyone, including their loved ones, at least in the beginning. Buddha departed from his son and wife at midnight. That kind of careless behaviour! Every relationship has a flaw in their eyes. You will be more exposed to disaster and farther from your ultimate goal, the more individuals you become attached to.

But if Buddha hadn't done this, how come we have witnessed one of the greatest philosophers?

I just wanted to write people in my books. Nothing less, nothing more.

Chapter-8

The Pandemic

We were unaware of the world. I was in my world and she was in hers. Her exams were over, and she was experiencing a more mature version of herself afterwards. My life had come to a halt.

Her life was on the verge of transforming at school, and she had already begun to transform herself as well. Although it made me feel sad, I was happy to see her embracing this new phase of life. I was happy for her because I wanted her to be able to make her own choices in life confidently. My complete focus was on working on my novel. I began working as a freelance writer.

Over time, her visits became less frequent. Her questions ended, and one day, I finally experienced the same event that usually happens to me. She mysteriously vanished from sight. She had opened up a whole new world in her life. I never contacted her via phone or text. Occasionally, I had the urge to inquire about her father's well-being, but I hoped she would update me herself.

I had no interest in discovering what was happening on Earth. I recently found a video of a Chinese woman enjoying bat soup. It was revolting, and prior to the virus reaching India, there was widespread criticism of China for its consumption habits, which is how these infections spread to humans.

Another theory was that the intentional attack of virus on the world by China. And it backfired on China first. Whatever it was, it just changed many things, and one of things was it took away many people's jobs, including mine. The company for which I was writing the articles suddenly vanished. I called my superior, and he was in a shock too. Our payments were on hold. They closed the website. For me, the payment—roughly INR25,000—was a substantial amount. With this money, I could have lived for months, but things have become worse.

Initially, I didn't believe it could turn into a pandemic. I believed it to be a flu that would pass in a few days or weeks. I believed that the TV videos depicting human fatalities were propaganda. The infected animals were cruelly being murdered and set on fire. Individuals were placed under quarantine. In the hospital, beds were filled and people were dying. Everything in life was chaotic. The immigrants fled their places of employment out of fear. Everyone was eager to go home.

'If we were to die in this pandemic, we would die in our home.' A person said in an interview with a reporter. He was walking to his home from Mumbai to Darbhanga, Bihar. A long caravan was on its way home.

My brother was jobless, too.

Our parents were worried about us, and we were about them.

*'We seek the route towards our family in time of crisis.'
I thought.*

Everything was suddenly different. She, however, did not text me or show up. Unexpectedly, priorities shifted. We had closed our doors after stocking our refrigerator with necessities. I made the conscious decision not to go home.

During the first part of lockdown, I really enjoyed it. I watched a Turkish TV series all day long. My brother was about to lose his mind. That's how he began smoking. I used to be a heavy smoker, but I had come down to one or two cigarettes a day.

A couple of days later, my cousin and his friend shifted to our house. They were working a little farther from us and, for the sake of saving money, they shifted to ours.

Now, two rooms had the occupancy of four. Abhi had cards. He taught me some advanced cards games and thus we found a time-killing sport.

What we did for the next one month, we got up in the morning, didn't care about bathe, shared our duties for the breakfast. Mostly, we ate bread, poha, and tea for the breakfast. Then we had our pack of cigarettes and here we go.

Usually, we would start playing this game around 10 am and get completely absorbed in it for four to five hours.

We had our duties in each of the home chores, from chopping onions to cleaning the toilet, had a common wallet for purchasing stuff. Only one provision store was opened nearby us. We usually cooked our meals in the afternoon. Who faces the trouble of cooking again and again?

The next task was to get busy with mobiles or take a nap.

We played cricket on the vacant ground at 4 pm, which was typically reserved for the hostel residents.

While playing cricket, I realized that how much fatigue had gathered in our muscles. We were growing old with lazy and loose body. I remembered my school days where we used to play the whole day during our holidays without a single mark of fatigue and tiredness. The starting week was too painful for us— to bowl, and to field, and to bat. I hit a shot off a full toss and felt like my arm had torn. I left the bat and sat on the ground.

The night routine was to play a movie, and for me to see my own stuff or to read. I have begun to enjoy this routine. There were no liabilities. The loan companies have provided the liberation on EMIs and waved off the penalties.

For me it was rejuvenating, I was so much happy. We were at the end of our savings, but I was fulfilled with joy, strength, and a tonne of happiness. I was so busy and caught up with everything that I nearly forgot about her. We barely used our phones. She had no interest in reaching out to me via phone or text.

When the lockdown was about to end, I got the message from her.

'Could you possibly come and pick me up? I need to return home, but because of my father's declining health, no one is available to pick me up. My mother wants me to stay, but I have to go with my brother. If you know someone, you can take the car from my home.'

Not uttering a greeting or inquiring about my actions or whereabouts, she said what was expected of her. She just asked for my help. She believed I was the sole person in her world capable of doing this. This message had just ended my lockdown officially because of the terrible intuition that I had developed inside my head. I almost forgot that she had a father situation.

'Call your mother and tell her I'm ready to come,' I said.

I asked for nothing else. There were rules for four wheelers to limit the capacity of the vehicle, and that's why I needed to go alone. Problem was not in going alone. The major problem was that I never drove a car for a purpose. My driving skills were not good. I didn't tell this thing to her or her mother.

With the keys in hand, I made my way towards Ghaziabad. I didn't have to cross through crowds or narrow roads, where I could sense the fear of collision or tyres getting off-road.

Each time I was shifting gears, the car jerked. After a few kilometres, I realized the clutch was not being properly pressed. When I crossed Mangalore, I finally put the car in its fifth gear.

I kept reminding myself that if anything went wrong, just hit the brakes. Luckily, nothing happened, and within four hours of travelling almost 170kms, I reached there. Due to Covid-19, I refrained from visiting her aunt's home. I just had one glass of water, and both of them sat in the car.

While turning the car, I hit one dustbin. Luckily, no one saw from the colony.

'I was certainly hoping that,' she said.

'It must've put the dent on the backside,' I said.

'We will see at home, just drive.'

I drove towards the home. Her brother was sitting in the back seat.

'You almost disappeared, didn't text or call?' I asked.

'The same could be said for you,' she said.

'Then how come you have thought about me to come here and pick you?' I asked.

'I knew that the lockdown must be going wonderful for you. That was the time that God provided for the people like you, so I thought I should ask for help from a cheerful person who can come here willingly,' she said.

I grinned.

'You drive terribly,' she said further.

'I'm new. Picking you is my first task ever,' I said.

'You should've seen my father's driving when he was fine. I never saw such a skilled driver like him. You will never feel a jerk or any sound of shifting gears in the car. Just pure comfort and smooth drive,' she said.

'One day, maybe I will drive like him.'

'No one could drive like him,' she said, and her eyes welled up.

'How's he?' I asked.

She didn't say a thing.

And in these rare instances, I never knew how to respond or inquire when someone is feeling conflicted.

'You're going to see him in a couple of hours. Just don't be sad,' I tried to console her and forgot to slow down the car on the breaker. The car faced a heavy jump.

'I'm sorry, sorry.'

'Just focus on the road,' she said.

For the next half an hour, we didn't talk. I kept focus on the road.

'I am not coming home for my father,' she finally broke the silence.

'Then?'

'I recently had a breakup and everything has just shattered inside me.'

'What! How? When did you…?' My tongue puzzled after hearing this.

'I know you wouldn't expect this from me. You always assumed me a girl of chaos, and I am. I never knew how to tell you. What would you think of me…and…I had a fear of losing you as a friend,' she said.

'That's not how things work with me,' I said.

'Means?'

'You owe me nothing. You don't have to brag your personal life to me. I'm okay with the truths and things you have showed. I'm just surprised. How come a girl with so much chaos managed a relationship?' I asked.

'One of my tuition mates. A horrible creature,' she said.

'He was thinking the same as you, even more,' I said.

'So, you are heartbroken and parallelly dealing with family issues,' I said further.

'I thought he would understand what I'm going through. He initially did, but when I came to my aunt's, a few days later, his behaviour changed. He called me crazy and sick,' she said.

'How old is he?' I asked.

'Same as me,' she replied.

'Blaming him won't work. Honestly, a boy your age might struggle to handle or take care of you. Their homes don't experience the same issues as yours. You need to handle it on your own,' I said.

'Long distance never works,' she said bluntly.

'If that would be true, then no one would love our soldiers. It's hard, but works for some people,' I said.

'You always have answers,' she said.

'Sometimes, I create them,' I said, chuckling.

'So, what did you do during the lockdown?' She asked.

'Played cards, cricket, smoked hundreds of cigarettes, movies, and you know.'

'There would be a lockdown for years if God ever listened to you.'

'I enjoyed it, and that's true. But for the past few days, I was missing cars and buses on the road. I was missing the crowd. Lockdown was like a vacation, but I hope things should be normal now.'

'What did you do at your aunt's?' I asked.

'Initially I felt good, but after a couple of days, it was hard for me. I was constantly missing my mother and ...my relationship ruined,' she said.

'It's okay, you can come to my place, just don't suffer too much,' I said.

Within an hour, we reached her home. The place where the car needed to park was out of my driving skills.

Luckily, his uncle was there, so he parked it. Her mother prepared tea for us. Her grandmother was there too. His father's grunting sound was echoing in the house. The ambience was miserable.

'How difficult this period would be for them', I considered.

'How did you manage his checkups during this time?' I asked her mother.

'God has made everything worse for me. It feels like his tests will never end,' she said.

'We pleaded to the doctors. The beds were full. Sometimes we had to wait for several hours and he had to lie down in the back seat of the car,' she said.

'I can understand.'

I sipped the tea, and returned to my room.

Next day, she came to our house, where we were about to celebrate my cousin's birthday. Just before cutting the cake, I saw her. I invited her, and we celebrated the birthday together.

'Let's go for a walk,' she requested.

We were walking on the road. She was quite upset for a reasonable reason.

'Why are you upset? You have bigger concerns at home. A teenager boy shouldn't be able to break you,' I said.

'I shared a deep bond with him,' she said.

'What's gone is gone.'

'I don't know, sometimes I feel there will always be troubles in my life,' she said.

'Why are you so desperate to make your life perfect at such a small age?' I said.

'I just want to leave home; I want to study in Ghaziabad. My aunt suggested I should get admission there,' she said.

'That's because of your father, but what do you want?' I asked her.

'I feel I don't belong here. I used to meet him here, and now he is not in my life, so I am thinking the way my aunt is thinking,' she said.

'Your anguish is only momentary, and you will soon find this area to be delightful once more. Are you prepared to leave this place and be apart from your family for at least three years because of this momentary pain?' I asked.

'Specifically, I want to convey that if you want to move, do so for a more compelling reason than merely a fleeting emotion,' I added further.

'But yesterday, my aunt has discussed my admission and paid a partial fee.'

'If you hurry, they will refund it.'

'My mum will definitely kill me; I am just horrible.'

'Here, I'm agree.'

We laughed together as I said it.

'They were talking about the transplant,' she said.

'His body won't accept; he is too weak. Transplant doesn't work like that. It's not like you just replaced an organ like battery and it will start working. Body takes a lot of time to accept it and for that, a lot of strength is needed,' I said.

'All of them are scared. They are thinking what would they reply if mum asked them to donate a part of their liver,' she said.

'It doesn't work like that. Everything has a procedure,' I said.

'My grandmother and one another lady have a match.'

'Doctor won't take from your grandmother, and that lady should volunteer herself.'

'I think many will match in your relations but no one will give. They will lie about their blood groups,' I said.

'They think they won't survive after donating,' she said.

'But your father needs strength first. Don't get me wrong, but what would happen if someone donated a fraction of his liver and things went wrong? That person will curse themselves. That's why they are stepping backwards,' I said.

'I don't know what we should do. My mother isn't thinking straight. She thinks everyone wants my father dead as soon as possible. That's why they are refusing to donate,' she said.

'I think all of your family members should be ready to donate, means at least for your mother's sake, the doctor won't approve the transplant until your father gets some strength. At least they should provide a comfort of being together for now,' I said.

'If the transplant doesn't happen soon; I'm afraid,' she said.

'Just pray for him.'

'When I reached home yesterday, and I saw my father, I freaked out. He has become a skeleton. He has nothing left in him. His yellow eyes seem to pop out from him anytime. He won't survive. I know,' she sobbed.

'We don't say things like that, Tanu,' I consoled her.

'Some kids have to leave their childhood soon; God has another plan for them.' I added.

Her phone rang.

'I have to go. It's urgent.'

Before I could ask something, she left. My heart just pumped an impulse. While I was consoling her, a fraction of her fear crept into me, making me sick and depressed. A girl who was about to lose his father and no one could do anything.

Everyone had known that he would not survive. That was the main reason that no one was ready to donate a fraction of their liver. All we could do was just praying to God to relieve him as soon as possible because of the pain he was in. He had tolerated more than enough.

Chapter-9

God's Plan

The lockdown was over, and things were returning to the normal pace quickly. A hustle and bustle over the street had showed its presence. Many businesses that had gone under immense loss were reopening in a hope of retaining their losses. Transport had begun too.

Next day, her mother called me and asked me for a wild herb called "Bhumi Amla" and sent me a picture and videos of the herb. She asked me if I could find it nearby. That plant can grow anywhere, and the best time is the rainy season which had begun already. It's small and has round shaped little amlas sticks to its tiny branches in a linear zig-zag pattern.

I saw the video and found out that the herb was very rare and widely used in Ayurvedic medicines for liver ailments. I roamed a few streets and found many plants. It was strange, though.

Before we know the importance of anything in the world, it's almost useless.

That plant was a trash, a weed, before I got to know the plant. I plucked ten whole plants and gave it to her mother, who was fighting the creator to save her husband at any cost.

'I will prepare chutney for him. It's a very good herb,' she said.

'Yeah, I recently got to know about that herb. Amazing results, as shown in the video,' I said.

'Where is Tanu?' I asked.

'In her room. Her result came out today, got 70 percent marks,' she said.

'That's very great news. She didn't inform me, though,' I said.

'That's why I called you here. Ask herself,' she said.

I went to her room. She was sitting there, numb.

'Hey broken angel, when were you going to tell me? After graduation?'

'I expected around 80. All of my friends have got above 80.'

'Everywhere you have to push your friends into your life. Your competition should not be them.'

'I thought you would be upset, too. That's why I didn't tell you.'

'I didn't expect 70, to be honest. Either they have done a loose marking or you have made a great effort within this miserable ambience.'

'There was no loose marking. My friends were expecting 90.'

'And why didn't you expect even 70 from me? Am I so dumb? You're treating me like they do,' she said.

'You're not dumb. Actually, if I were you, I would've failed in at least one subject. You have gone through a lot,' I said.

'You are dumber, that means,' she said after a pause, and we laughed.

Her mother came with sweets. Before they could give me, I picked one and offered them first.

'It's your victory. Now your daughter will pursue graduation. You should be proud of her,' I said.

'Yes, next week she is going to shift Ghaziabad to her aunt's home for her studies. She won't be able to study here properly. If she hadn't been in this environment, she would've gotten more marks,' she said.

'Is she ready to......move on there?' I asked.

'Yes, she has already paid 10,000 in advance for the fee,' she said.

'Oh, that's good. I would say that just think thoroughly before getting admission to any college,' I said.

Tanu remained silent throughout. I assumed she was in a dilemma. Her mother sincerely wanted her to study outside, but Tanu wrestled with whether to ask her mother to transfer school or simply give up on her own ambitions.

'I need to go. If you need any help regarding counselling or college, just call me,' I said.

Her grandmother was sitting beside her father.

I went back to my room.

'Can you actually convince my mother that I actually don't want to go there?' She texted.

'I could've, but it seems she herself wants to send you outside for your own good,' I replied.

'I can't ditch my family at this time,' she wrote.

'You shouldn't. Just talk to your mother when she is calm,' I replied.

'I will try, but if things didn't go right, then you will have to interfere for sure,' she wrote.

I was searching for my phone charger and, like always, I didn't find it. I was getting upset with myself because I couldn't seem to stay organized.

'Just do as I said,' I replied in a bit rudeness.

A few minutes later:

'I don't need anything. Thank you,' she wrote.

And that was expected of her. She must have thought of herself as a burden to me.

'I lost my charger.' I wrote.

'Sorry for the interruption, but I won't be able to come to you. I can't tolerate more rudeness,' she replied.

The circumstances in which she was breathing were already traumatic, and I should have realized that she couldn't handle anything that would even slightly increase her pain.

'I'm sorry, it was just my charger,' I wrote.

'Ask your cousin. He might know,' she replied.

And she was right. It was under his pillow and he was lying above it.

'How did you know the charger was here?' My cousin asked me.

'Where would it be? You use your phone almost the whole day,' I said.

'That girl is into you, somehow I feel,' he said.

'We should not breach the area in which we are not experts in,' I said.

'Only she saw me carrying your charger the previous day,' he said.

'She might be an excellent observer, just don't make it a big deal out of a charger.'

She came to me for three days during her therapy sessions, which she believed only I could provide for her. I always try to tell her what she needed to hear. Sometimes she laughed, cried, or sometimes she just didn't say a word.

Fourth day, her mother called me.

'Would it be workable for you to make arrangements for two individuals to donate blood? We need blood urgently,' she said.

I, with my cousin, immediately went to the hospital she mentioned.

Both of us donated the blood. Her uncle was there.

Tanu's father was lying down in the bed, unconscious. The syringe was delivering blood into his veins. His hands became pale and appeared to shrink. His hand had several noticeable puncture marks. There, Tanu's mother sat in silence.

The fear that I didn't want to be true was coming true. I could see the truth. He had little time left, and all I wanted God to be fair to him in his last moments. The most important thing, hope, was now gone from his mind.

I came to my room, and within an hour, Tanu called me.

'They are taking my father to Noida. His condition has become worse. Couldn't accept blood,' she said.

'I'm coming to your home,' I said.

Upon arriving at her home, I found her grandmother, and aunt present. I was in her room where her brother and two more friends of hers were seated on the sofa.

While sitting there, I wanted them to engage in any conversation and we were talking about Tanu's college admittance, and at other times, I was offering a few lines of advice to her friends. We talked about various topics in our usual way. I refrained from letting them believe what they would learn in a few hours. Tanu hoped her father could recover in a hospital with better amenities. Her uncle contacted me. I did not know where he got my number from.

'He passed away, just make the environment calm till we come,' he said.

I almost froze. She was right behind me.

'What happened? What did uncle say?' She asked.

'He is in the ICU, under the supervision of more skilled doctors,' I blurted, before she could ask anything.

She came along with me. We were on the first floor and the ground floor was almost full of women. They were sitting on the roof.

The wind on that day was harsh and prickly. The night was filled with an eerie silence and overwhelming fear. I was examining all of them from a completely different perspective. Her brother was engaged in playing with a Rubik's cube. Tanu was chatting with her friends, indulging in gossip about something highly unlikely to occur and that could cease at any moment. A significant shift was about to occur in this house.

A phone rang on the ground floor, and a few seconds later, I heard glass cracking. Then, a voice dropped into our ears, sounding horrible and wailing. After a few seconds, the voice escalated its pitch. Her brother spat up whatever he had eaten out of fear. Tanu heard me mutter that her father had passed away. She grabbed me and one of her friends and began to cry. My whole body went numb. My legs and hands had stopped working and were trembling. The terrible pitched voice of the sobbing women shocked her brother so much that he dropped to the ground.

'Your brother,' I screamed.

Tanu slapped his brother. We had taken him to the bathroom where she cleaned his face and made him rinse.

She was constantly crying. Her brother was crying too, not because of the news but because of that scary ambience.

I picked him up and lay down with him on the bed. He was not ready to leave me. I didn't let him. The crying voices got slow down after an hour. A couple of women came, and again, the crying voices just pitched our ear. He puked again.

Tanu was sitting beside us. She was cleaning. Her nose turned crimson as she was repeatedly wiping her tears.

'He is now at peace; he is not suffering now. Pain has ended,' I said to her.

She didn't say a thing.

'We are without a father now; the shield has gone. He left us open and now we are more vulnerable,' she sobbed and said.

The ambulance had come. Her exhausted mother came outside and grabbed her granny. I could witness the paramount of grief a lady bore when she becomes a widow. She had every reason to cry. For the past two years, she had turned every rock for her beloved husband. Even in his last moments, she was searching for the herbs. Her dedication towards him left no void. Tanu had gone to her mother, and I was with her brother. He was utmost terrified. I was shushing him.

'Don't worry,' I kept saying to him.

It was late at night and such places couldn't be left without performing the proper rituals. Everyone was exhausted. No one was crying now. Their eyes had stopped streaming with tears.

Tanu came to me.

'Is it okay if I take him to our mother?' She asked.

'Don't do that. He is scared and hardly got his nap.'

'Everything crumbled. My plans and future.'

'Just don't think of anything. Now is not the moment.'

The birds began to trill as morning approached. Someone put in a tea order for everyone. When I peered out the channel window, I saw that her father's body had been covered in a white shroud and placed close to the gate entry.

Tanu brought tea for me, which was a must for the moment; otherwise, my head was going to explode.

She had stopped crying. Nobody cries all the time; our bodies are not made to do that. We weep till the agony is gone, and then we cease. The person's memory comes back and goes away over time. As a result, we cry for a while, and as the pain passes, we feel normal. We grieve every time a memory returns, and we keep doing this until we are resilient enough to handle this sorrow. After that, we simply recall the person without crying since we have become accustomed to their memories.

The purohit had come.

'I saw the face of my father. It seems that he is going to wake up after sleep and ask me for something to bring,' she said.

'He will always be with you,' I said.

'He will curse me. I always argued with him.'

'He won't curse you.'

'I am going to miss him badly,' she said and sobbed.

'Just be your mother's strength. She will need her family more than ever.'

'I'm going to her.'

'I will be back in one hour. Your cousin is taking care of your brother.'

Both of us came down. There was an immense crowd that gathered already. Everyone who knew him was there, his coworkers, too. The guest ladies were consoling her mother. The atmosphere was tense.

I went to my room and within half an hour; I completed the daily chores of mine but didn't take a bath. By the time I reached there, they were preparing her father for cremation. The van had come and her mother was screaming and women were trying to hold her. I saw the bruise marks on her arm of broken bangles. Tanu's brother was with her uncle. He saw me and came to me.

Saying farewell is never easy. In the end, what a person has done with his life is irrelevant. What counts is his departure and the void that he is leaving in his footprints. Even though he was sick and caused suffering for everyone, he will be missed terribly. The place where he rested holds a special significance that will be missed. The 44-inch TV, air conditioner he ordered last month, and medication box would all clearly display his presence. Even though the man was no longer with them, his memory will continue to live on in his house.

Everyone was in tears. Tanu was holding her mother. The body was put in the van. I was in the van too, sitting beside her brother. He was still scared. His eyes and cheeks were swollen.

At shamshaan, the sight was quite pathetic and miserable. Three pyres were already burning. The purohit told them to do final rituals. Her brother was called. They rubbed some herbs over his father's body, including ghee. The last time I saw his swollen stomach, the marks of holes which were used to drain excess water were visible.

How terrible the scene was! A twelve-year-old, who was supposed to be in school at this time or in the playground, was revolving around his dead father, having a burning wood in his hand. A burned coal from the ashes of another pyre hit his leg, he stopped, and started crying. His uncle came and helped him complete the ritual. He didn't know a thing, and he didn't want to provide the salvation to his father through that wood stick because he was scared and terrified. They were yelling and forcing him to perform the final rites. After setting the pyre on fire, he came directly to me. We were sitting in a waiting room. The Holy Ganga was passing by. Both of us were watching his father burn. Half an hour later, all of us were called and purohit asked us for two minutes of silence for the soul to rest in the peace. Then we returned.

I directly came back to my room, had a bath, and sat in my chair.

'Everything would change for her now.' I thought.

I made no attempt to call or text her. My intention was for her to mourn completely. I wanted her to miss her father as much as she could. It was my desire for her to be with her mother and brother. I wanted her to cry in the corner.

Chapter-10

A New Reality

On the fourth day, she came to me. Her swollen face said everything. It seemed that she had cried enough and now she wanted to breathe some air.

'My mother is extremely in pain. She is angry with everyone for not stepping in to donate the liver,' she said.

'But why now?' I asked.

'She couldn't see his vacant side of the bed; she misses him badly,' she said.

'Time will heal everything.'

'Another thing.'

I looked at her strangely. I gazed upon her guilty face, like she wanted to confess something.

'Has something happened to you?' I asked.

'No, my father had doubts about you. He kept asking my mother about you and your frequent visits to our home.'

'I hope your mother had clarified everything.'

'She did, indeed.'

'You're hiding something.'

I saw her dry eyes getting wet again. A few drops of tears fell down on the ground.

'Tanu, just tell.' I said, forcefully.

'A lady.... a lady visited our home last week. Almost the same age as my mother. She has a son. She sat in the chair and cried for almost half an hour, then she sat beside my father's head and rubbed his forehead. My father put his hand over hers and fell asleep. Then, with one hand covering her weeping mouth, she sprang up and rushed out of the house.' she said.

'So, what do you want to say?'

'I assume you're smart enough to guess.'

'Your father had an affair?'

'Beside mourning and consoling each other, now everyone is accusing him of being unfaithful to my mother.'

'Does anyone have any proof?'

'There could be other theories, too. Maybe your father had helped her in her needy time, and she had an emotional spot for him. Why start with negatives?' I asked.

My phone beeped. It was a message from the loan app, showing my outstanding amount and the legal action that could be initiated if I didn't pay at least one EMI. This message hit me like my hangover had ended.

'It could be an affair, too. Can't it?'

'What would happen if they arrived at my house? They will embarrass my parents.' I thought about the loan collection team.

'I should go, I think,' she said and before she could get up, I grabbed her hand for a second and then left.

'Sorry, something came up in my mind,' I said.

'Your father didn't have any affair; how could it be? For the last two years, he was on medications. He has already given you a decent life, always came to you at night. How come? And most importantly, instead of learning his best memories after his demise, we are discussing this shit. This is awkward for me; I couldn't imagine that we are discussing an affair of a person whose soul just left the earth. It's bad,' I said.

'These things are being discussed in my home by women. My mother is burning from the inside. What should I do? I wanted to memorise him in peace. Peace has gone from my home. People are such motherfuckers that they can't let us mourn in the peace. Women come and faked their cries for two minutes, and afterwards, gossip start. They discuss everything except the memories of my father. They are discussing the open sewers in the city and the smell of shit,' she said.

'It is only for a few days that they will come. Just bear them,' I said.

'Let's go somewhere,' I suggested.

'Anywhere' I said.

'Amrapur Ghat,' she suggested.

I took her scooty, and we parked it near the big Om. We sat at the bank of the Ganga.

'This place is just a remedy for me. It can soothe anyone's soul,' I said and almost forgot that she was going through the trauma.

'I still couldn't digest that my father is no more. It seems like he would by lying down in the bed, and mother would give him some herbs. It's too hard to accept,' she said.

I realized my mistake.

'I want you to memorise him and just try to accept that he is in cosmos, but his memories will be with you forever.'

Her eyes were filled with tears. Tears were flowing incessantly. I lightly touched her shoulder to remind her I was by her side. We had our feet dipped in the river. Holy Ganga was constantly receiving her tears as an offering.

'May Ganga Maa blessed her and provide her every comfort.' I thought.

Then she wiped her tears and nose.

'My mother refused me to take admission in Ghaziabad. I will go either to any university in Roorkee or to a nearby college,' she said.

'That's good.'

'Mummy will look after the catering business after papa.'

'And you will help her along with your studies.'

'I need one more help from you.'

'Just ask.'

'I need to drive my car to transport the stuff for our catering. I want you to be my instructor.'

'You have seen me; I drive like a beginner.'

'But you know how to… and it would be a good idea for you to enhance your driving skills too.'

'But we need a place and the time.'

'We have both. I won't come until the Tehervee. After that, we will start our driving lesson. Let's go. I have to be at my home.'

As I was sitting in my chair, I was thinking everything about her again. The lockdown was just a dream. A feeling of unease was just waving through my veins. I was not thinking about myself. The message of my pending EMI was telling me I needed to work on myself, too. I was just imagining myself sitting in her car and instructing her how to drive.

I have made a detailed plan for myself, outlining tasks that need to be completed at different job sites in the coming days. My resume was ready. I was heavy-hearted because a debt made me do things I buried a long time ago. The thought of looking for another job was something

I never wanted to experience again. I had a desire to engage in reading, watching, and writing. I felt frustrated with myself. My anger towards the system was intense. My phone was constantly bombarded with fraudulent calls.

I searched for freelancing jobs. Three recruiters called me and offered me to writing job, and before I could say yes, they asked me to relocate. No one was ready to give me a job without relocating. For a couple of seconds, I thought about moving for one year, just to earn money, but I was so desperate to give her a driving lesson. I knew if tell her I got a job in Pune city, she wouldn't ask me to stay. She will find another way to learn how to drive. But I didn't want that. I postponed the idea of the job and relocating.

And asking money from friends is cool, initially. Friends do help selflessly; I agree, but what I've learnt from my past lessons is that money can easily ruin your relationships. You borrow money from your friend and just casually he calls you, what you would think at the very first? That what if he wants his money back? And if you don't have money at that time, you would certainly hesitate to pick his call and hence friendship is ruined. Keep money out of your personal relationships.

And I have my firm opinion on that, if you want to make your relationships healthy, just be a giver first. Like, if you're on a trip with your friends, just make your portion a little big for the entire budget. And if you can't do that, just cancel the trip. They may convince you again, if they are your good friends, still cancel it. If they come to you and put you in the car forcibly, then you can repay them later. Otherwise, never be in anyone's debt. Don't be a borrower in the first place. That's why I learned to live on a minimum budget, on essential things.

I learned that loans make your hair go grey earlier than a low salary.

'I am obligated to repay my loan in any way possible.'

A WhatsApp message came to me. It was her. I opened it, and I was called to attend her father's last rites, i.e. Tehervee.

Once I attended the holy last rites, I greeted her mother. I didn't get the chance to greet earlier. She was still in tremendous pain. I tried to console her.

'Today, he has found his way to the next life. He is free from pain and attachments,' I said.

She just nodded her head. Her eyes welled up. Tanu was sitting beside her.

'Come to us tomorrow evening,' she said.

'I will, for sure,' I said.

Next day, I was sitting with them. Tanu had prepared tea for us.

'When he was dead, and these women came to snatch my beautiful bangles which I bought for myself. That was terrible. When these women took away all his clothes and my make-up stuff, that was terrible. When they wiped the sindoor and advised me to wear faded clothes for my entire life, that was terrible. At that moment, I wanted to kill them all. I wanted to beat them until they begged for death. How come they may take away someone's belongings without asking that person? What if I wanted to keep some stuff from my husband as a memory? They didn't let me do it and they all call it customs,' she almost roared with anger.

I was astonished.

'How brutal is that? Are these filthy practices still being carried out by people? Can't a widow wear something good for herself?' I asked.

'These women, they won't let us rise. A widow is a labelled woman. If today I wear a pretty dress, they will gossip. They will long think and they would conclude eventually that I've had an affair. A pretty dress shows that I want to seduce a man,' she said.

'Even my mother, the lady which gave birth to me and raised me until my marriage, says that I should focus on spiritual TV channels and charity works,' she grieved.

'It feels like I don't have my own identity. It feels like I'm just a scrap without my husband,' she added further.

'You don't have to listen to them; you have two beautiful kids and you should move on. And the catering business will keep you busy,' I said.

'Give her proper driving lessons. I need her to be perfect, like her father. I don't want to beg for any help from anyone,' she said.

Tanu put the car's key in my hand. I gently ignited the engine and, at a low pace, we reached at the destination: The BHEL Ground.

There was one additional person who was undergoing a driving lesson at that place. Actually, it wasn't a field, but rather an empty area next to the field. There are some potholes, broken bricks, and stones scattered around, as well as a couple of fallen trees. It was the learners who built the trail of the track. However, on the opposite side, there was the State Bank of India, and a few customers of the bank have also chosen to park their vehicles here.

So, we had a natural obstacle contained place. We switched seats.

'Seatbelt first,' I said.

At the very first, I briefly told her about gears and shifting, which she already knew because of her father.

'Just ignore gears for now. Learn it in my style. Remember, ABC from right to left. Acceleration, Brake and Clutch. And the most important paddle is the brake paddle. If your brain goes numb, just hit the brake,' I said.

'The clutch pedal is the second most important pedal. If you press it, then the engine will be free and the car would behave like a four-wheeled cart. And when you gently lift it, the engine takes control of the tyres. Never, ever lift it in a rush, otherwise the car will feel a jerk.'

'The accelerator, or race paddle, is the third most important. Completely press down on the clutch pedal with your left foot and place your right foot on the brake pedal.'

'Now put it in first gear. Release brake paddle and gently release clutch paddle.'

I had expected her making an error in her initial try, but to my surprise, she executed my instructions flawlessly and released the clutch with such elegance that the car began to move effortlessly.

'Very impressive. Let it go, let it go. Just keep it on the track, use steering. And gently speed up it,' I said.

She pressed the race paddle, and the car caught speed.

'Brake, brake.' I said aloud. She hit the brake, and the car stopped with a jerk.

'Race paddle is soft. We only have to touch it. Don't force press it.'

'Again,' I said.

She learned quietly for two hours. She wanted to learn immediately, and she was learning quite faster than me.

Next day, we started earlier and now she was shifting gears and making sharp turns. Her feet learned the ABC concept.

And the next day, after two hours of learning, she turned the car towards the main road.

'No, no…. not so soon,' I said and tighten my seat belt.

'You're not even eighteen,' I shouted.

'I'm eighteen,' she laughed while driving. She took an inside road which meets at the Ranipur More, one of the densest roads in the city. She had no fear, but she couldn't figure out the precise estimate to protect the car's sides. Anyone can guess that some amateur was driving.

As we drove, a cop spotted us, but before he could stop us, she skilfully navigated past him. We passed by Shankar Ashram and Arya Nagar Chowk, and now we had to navigate through the narrow streets of Ambedkar Nagar to reach her home. The situation became tense when we encountered an approaching pickup truck. Even I felt anxious about driving through these cramped streets. Eventually, we came to a halt, and I couldn't help but worry about what would happen next. How would we find a way out?

To make matters worse, the car wasn't parked properly, causing the truck driver to become furious as it obstructed the already narrow passage. A crowd gathered behind us, further adding to the tension. I hesitated to take the wheel, feeling incapable of maneuvering out of this predicament. However, she took a chance and shifted the car into reverse. Peeking her head out of the window, she signalled for those behind us to move back. With determination, she put in fifteen minutes of effort and successfully freed the car from its tight spot.

Relieved, we continued our journey and arrived home safely, with no damage or accidents. Finally, a smile stretched across my face, mirroring the joy she felt as she giggled. Her mother watched proudly from the terrace as we parked the car ourselves. In the evening, we enjoyed a cup of tea, savouring the triumph of overcoming the challenging situation.

'I didn't expect her to learn so fast. Her father would be so proud of her,' her mother said.

'Actually, me too. She is a fast learner,' I said.

'How many days will she need more?' She asked.

'It's all about practicing. She has learned the basics…one more thing. While hitting brakes, don't press clutch paddle,' I said to Tanu.

'But the engine gets shuts off,' she replied.

'When you apply the brakes, the engine restricts the movement of the tires. It controls the rotation of the tires. It acts as an opposing force. Only press the clutch when the car is about to stop, otherwise the car will continue to move because of its momentum,' I said.

'Physics,' she said.

'Basic momentum law,' I said.

I sipped the tea and then came back to my room. I was constantly thinking about how different she was. In a period of three days with an amateur instructor, she drove to her home. I could've understood if she were a boy, but despite being a girl, she outranked many boys. For one second, it seemed that her father was inside her and instructing her to drive. But that was fantastic. A fearless act.

Chapter-11

A Widow's Wail

'I surprised you today,' she texted me, followed by a smiling emoji.

'You almost killed me today. You could've taken a couple of more days,' I replied.

'In a couple of days, I would be better,' she wrote.

After a very long time, I was browsing Instagram and discovered that everyone is too busy entertaining or lecturing the rest of the globe. The more I scrolled, the more I realized I needed it. The show seemed to drag on endlessly. After experiencing a lump on my head for an hour, I closed the app. I realized that in today's society, there are individuals who choose to be alone in front of the camera. Creating videos is the type of therapy they specialize in. I will always remain uninterested in Facebook, Instagram, and Snapchat. I feel disconnected from myself because of them, and it frustrates me. They take us from us.

Although I understood they were still in the grieving process, I wanted to ask her whether we could continue our red scooty ride. I had to wait for her to move on to her next venture and I needed something to utilize my time. I invested myself in a new season, Vikings.

The ancient, fierce warriors of Norway. The season was shot so beautifully that it compels you to dive into their era of bloodshed. Their raids and looting on England and how they have plotted under their magnificent and brilliant leader Ragnar Lothbrock and her shield maiden wife Lagertha. She reminded me of our lady warrior, The Queen of Jhansi. They worshipped Odin and had a belief that after death, all of them will be assembled in the great hall of Valhalla, i.e. their heaven, where they would feast with their ancestors. What a beautiful and magnificent concept in a slightly different way. Besides, they were more violent. The most beautiful encounter wasn't among people but among faiths, because in England, all were Christians and they had their faith in Jesus Christ. Ragnar slowly believes that there was no God and that man was the master of his own fate. He says to his slave priest Athelstan, "I hope that someday our gods can become friends."

Then I saw her message on the screen.

'Today, the mother received a phone call from that woman, and she has been crying nonstop ever since,' she wrote.

'Gently ask her. She's only got you now,' I replied.

'She said this doesn't concern me. I shouldn't hear this,' she wrote.

'I know she will definitely tell you if you would come here. She needs an adult to talk,' she texted again.

'But why would she tell me her personal matters?' I asked.

'You are a decent guy in her mind,' she wrote.

'I would come earlier in the evening before your driving lesson,' I wrote.

'Okay.'

That's how my mind works. I was virtually in the Norway and England just before her text, and now I just landed here again. That's the switching between my real and virtual world. I get lost when I watch some movie or season. I downloaded a ton of wallpapers of Ragnar since he was my new hero. He became a philosopher. They had their boats and a compass with a rage and fury, and in order to seek Valhalla, they raided many places and looted everything.

'Don't come in the same t-shirt,' she added further.

A smile came upon my face. I wore my brother's brown striped t-shirt. I didn't let him know. My brother is one of the guys who never shares his stuff. He is so possessive about everything he owns.

I visited her house. Her mother had swollen eyes. It seemed as if she suddenly halted her crying. I didn't inquire. I gazed at the wedding photo of her and her husband. The incredible and ideal couple. Tanu sat silently next to her mother. The TV was occupied with her brother playing a video game. The shooting video game he was playing filled the entire house with echoes.

'Prepare tea,' she said to Tanu.

'No, I've just had my tea,' I lied. She eyed-ordered her.

'Just have some with us. At least you are coming regularly,' she said.

'Just don't be so hard on yourself.' I tried to console her.

'His death revealed something that was too hard to bear. It's traumatic,' she said.

'What happened? You could share if you want to,' I said.

'He had an affair. He loved her more than me. I was just a societal responsibility for him,' she revealed, and tears just burst out of her eyes.

'Are you sure? I hope this must be a misunderstanding,' I said.

'She came here a week before his death, didn't bother to ask anything from me, and just sat beside his head. She rubbed his head… and…'

'And?'

'She was doing what I should have been doing,' she laughed with pain.

'He saw her and gently called her name and asked her to rub more. And she was rubbing and crying. My husband was being taken care of by a lady who was crying for him and I never knew because I always trusted him,' she grieved.

'And no one knows about this? Not even his friends?' I asked.

'This is the problem. I recently found out that everyone knew except me. The man I always loved was not mine, and that disgusts me. I lost everything. Despite being thirty-eight, I appear to be fifty years old. I have become disconnected from my womanhood. Even though I tirelessly took care of him, all I am now is a lifeless corpse. And what did I receive in return? I have fought with God. He could have died much earlier, but I prolonged his life and yet I can't find any peace. Every night, I curse him,' she erupted with the whole fire.

'If everyone knew, then why didn't any of them tell you about this?' I asked.

'Had any of them fulfilled their moral duty, you wouldn't be facing this. That's painful,' I said.

'There are no morals for men in our society. A man does what he pleases, but a woman has to think about the entire reputation of the family like she is the only one responsible for it,' she said.

'For nineteen years, I had complete devotion to the seven promises I took while doing the seven *feres*. But this man, the only man I loved, cheated on me. My whole married life was a lie, and he had gone without even fulfilling his duties as a father. How would I manage the home and kids both?' She added further.

Tanu was tensed too, but she didn't know how to console her mother. If she had been a few years older, she would have performed it more effectively.

'I would say just one thing, since he has been cremated now, so every faulty memory of him should be cremated too. Don't just invite pain. Cursing those people who have gone from here wouldn't bring any good fortune. It's hard, I know, but this is the only viable option. Otherwise, there is no way you can find your peace,' I said.

She was giving a head nod. We took a few slow sips of the ginger-flavoured tea that Tanu brought.

'Today, I will drive the entire way,' she said.

'Of course, you should,' I said.

'Just drive carefully and listen to your instructor,' her mother said.

Initially, we attached a learning label to the rear windshield of the vehicle, after which she turned on the engine and we drove to our residence. Similar to my previous experience, she broke a dustbin while leaving those crowded streets, but we were able to flee unnoticed. She completed the BHEL round by herself. She had a desire to drive across the entire Haridwar. We ended up back where we began, on the starting field.

'I forgot to tell you something,' she said.

'Just focus on driving first. We can discuss later.' I wanted her not to lose her grip or fall into any type of conversation right now.

'I wanted to say that there is one more famous Siddhpeeth temple here—Goddess Sureshvari Devi,' she said.

'Oh yes, I have heard about that temple. It's in the jungle, in Rajaji National Park,' I said.

'This is the way to go there,' she showed me a trackway which was going towards the jungle.

'We will go there someday,' I said.

'We will bring mother,' she said.

'She will witness your fine skill of driving,' I said.

'You're lost. It seemed you wanted to say something but couldn't dare to,' she said.

She sensed I was about to say something.

'Do you want to remember your father as a cheater or guilty?' I asked.

'Never. I remember only his wonderful memories,' she said.

'I hope someday your mother remembers him like this,' I said.

'She didn't tell you the full story,' she said.

'She has told enough,' I said.

'My mother is a widow and deprived. She went to my father's catering business to inquire about a job, and once she was hired as a receptionist, a few other nefarious staff members began making advances on her. Upon discovering this, the father asked HR to move her to the HR division. She grew closer to my father as a result. He and my mother used to argue a lot back then because of his binge drinking. Thus, he discovered someone who could put up with him—even when he's drunk. He used to tell Mother that he had been staying at the firm whenever he drank too much and would go to sleep at her house,' she said.

'So, you want to say that he didn't leave your mother? He just supported and found his love in another woman too,' I said.

'Yes, you can conclude this,' she said.

'Your mother is young. Isn't she thinking about another marriage?' I asked.

'Never put that idea in her mind. She is vulnerable at this time and people who are against us want that. Our family would be ruined,' she said with a hard voice.

'What if your mother wants this? Won't you think about her happiness?' I asked.

'We are heading home,' she didn't answer my question and turned the car towards her home.

We were moving in silence. It was confusing to me why she was so concerned by this question. I said nothing at all. It wasn't wise of me to ask. They were still in a state of grief. I stepped out of the car as she was parking it and ignited my bike. I couldn't help but feel something inside of me and not want to talk to her about anything. She paused for a few moments, expecting me to say something, but I remained silent.

Her mother was waiting for me to visit her house as she watched us from the first floor. I just disappeared, and I lay down on my bed right away. Her mother must have questioned her about what had occurred, I was sure. Neither did she call or text me. It was utterly strange and repulsive. I couldn't decide which was more disgusting – her disregard for my opinion of her mother's remarriage or my behaviour towards her. At this point, they might have been questioning whether they could trust me. Her mother might feel uncomfortable disclosing her husband's secret to me.

I picked up my phone.

'You are right. I shouldn't have said this,' I texted.

'You shouldn't ditch me in front of my mother. As she is already handling many people and things, you should have not given her a reason to worry. She asked me about what had happened,' she replied.

'I'm really sorry. Tell her that my stomach was upset, and I needed to hurry. You should've made up something by now,' I wrote.

'That won't work. She has already read my face,' she texted.

'What am I doing?'

'I only wanted to know your opinion, and you ignored me like I am imposing something on you.' I texted.

'I've ignored you many times in the past, made my face and ghosted you. How come today's ignorance was so penetrative to your mind?' She asked.

And that was absolutely right. How come her behaviour affected me today? How come I got so emotionally carried that I had to ditch her? Had something changed inside of me? Whatever that was, was not right. I decided to go to her to home to make amends. I didn't inform her. Her mother was talking to her neighbour on the street. She saw me and ignored me. That was penetrative. I was in a position whether I should return to my place or go to hers. While my mind was stuck, I was busy searching the locket of my key inside both of my pockets just to avoid my feeling guilty. But I could only search for my keys for a couple of seconds, maximum. So, I had to find another side hustle. I picked up my phone and dialled my mother number and then I cut the call. The things I was doing felt like absolute madness. Her mother finally ended her gossip and came to me.

'Has Tanu said something offensive to you?'

'No, actually, my stomach had some problem, so I had to rush to the home to take pills,' I falsify her assumptions.

'She is upside, and tensed,' she said.

'I enlightened something inside her about her future and she is worried. And…she is terribly missing her father,' I said.

'Come.'

I was sitting in the chair. She called Tanu, and she came outside.

'He is your teacher and instructor, that behaviour of yours towards him isn't valid. He can scold you; bear it and learn from it,' she said to Tanu.

'What the hell!'

Tanu didn't speak. Inside her head, she had a jumble of emotions. She returned to her own room.

'She will obey,' she said.

'How are her driving lessons going?' She asked further.

'We will go to the temple, Sureshwari Devi. And Tanu will drive and take us there,' I said.

'We could go there; it's been a long time. We will go on Sunday.'

'What about Keshav? Is he all right?'

'I want him to grow sooner. He has a lot of responsibility.'

'Things will work out in their own flow; I would advise against pressuring him to mature too quickly to avoid turning him into an unhappy adult.'

'I feel tired. I just don't want to be responsible anymore. What had I got for being responsible? An unfaithful husband?'

'You have fulfilled your part. What he has done has gone with him. Just try to liberate him, and at the very first, forgive him. It's for your inner peace.'

She was lost. You can't erase someone's memory.

Visiting her home and consoling her mother had become a regular habit for me, as I also took on the role of a guardian to take care of her. Sometimes I visited there more than once in a single day. I had stopped being her tutor. I noticed a change in her behaviour towards me as she became more open and honest. She would visit my room regularly, and sometimes she would even bring chicken to cook. Occasionally, my brother would cast us an icy glare and simply pretend as if we didn't exist. Whatever it was, everything went without a hitch.

She drove all of us to Sureshvari Devi on Sunday.

Step into the Sureshwari Devi Temple and instantly find yourself in a peaceful sanctuary that offers an escape from the outside world. In a quiet hideaway on the fringes of the green forest, this place offers a sanctuary where you can unwind and forget about the hustle and bustle of the lively city.

When you visit, you'll walk on paths surrounded by trees and nature. It's so quiet, you can hear birds singing and leaves rustling. The temple itself is old and has a special feeling because so many people have come here to pray. This temple is dedicated to Goddess Durga and is located on Soorkoot Mountain. It's surrounded by beautiful forests which keep it cool, even when it's hot outside. The temple area is very peaceful and you can see the forest as you go in.

The temple is situated atop a gentle hill, requiring you to ascend a set of stairs to reach the main area. Within the premises, you will discover a spacious courtyard adorned with a majestic and age-old banyan tree. As you step inside the primary temple, you will encounter intricately crafted idols of Mata Sureshwari Devi. Additionally, nestled within the courtyard, there is a separate shrine dedicated to Lord Shiva, featuring a sacred Shiva Linga and statues portraying Shiva's divine family.

If you continue climbing the stairs up the hill, you will come across another Kali Mata temple. Not only does it provide a bird's-eye perspective of the surrounding area, but it also occasionally offers the opportunity to catch a glimpse of wildlife. This place offers a peaceful and serene environment, providing an escape from the busy and chaotic city life, allowing you to reconnect with the beauty of nature. This spot would be ideal for anyone who is seeking a retreat, looking to deepen their connection to their faith, or simply has a love for nature. The Rudraksha Tree, standing before the temple, caught our attention and held it. Our intention was to gather a few; however, we were informed that it was forbidden to disrupt the sanctity of the tree. While visiting the temple is an important aspect of the experience, there is so much more to explore and discover.

Chapter-12

The Devil

After our time at the temple, we made our way back and felt tired. Her mother insisted me to get some rest. They had a big screen TV, so sometimes I would continue my episodes or recent movies on their television. However, her grandmother wasn't at the same pace as they were to me. She whispered something into her mother's ear. I was foreseeing it anyhow. When Tanu told me about that situation, I assured her everything would be fine. I became so popular with their relatives. Everyone knew me. Some knew me as a good person and some had doubts.

A wedding was approaching in her family, so she requested me to go shopping with her. She wanted to purchase a dress. After we entered the store, I quickly grabbed my spot and opened Instagram. After entering a trial room, she emerged. I looked at her clothing. Just like a caterpillar undergoes a metamorphosis and becomes a butterfly, the girl who used to wear loose clothing transformed into a beautiful young woman. She approached me.

'How am I looking? Didn't you notice?'

'Gorgeous.' I bluntly replied.

The guy at the shop was watching us and smiling. I didn't know what he concluded, but it was a weird and good combo of my emotions. Despite my heart's strong desire, I was not prepared to fall in love with her. I was receiving calls and messages from loan recovery companies the entire day to repay my debt, so I didn't want to add any additional strings with her. I didn't want her to be a part of my misdeeds. No plans, no promises—just letting things happen. She didn't question me again after spotting my mood. We went to her house after she made her outfit choice.

'What's it that bothering you so much? You could share it with me. Maybe I could ease your burden,' she said.

'Nothing,' I replied.

'Please, I wanted to be your problem listener, like you are to me,' she said.

'While I can offer you the solution to your problem, I am not the person who can resolve it. As you have seen too, my life is a mess. I want to be a master of my fate, but life wants something else from me,' I said.

'You're in a financial crisis, I know, but things will improve soon.'

'I can't share with you about the exact crisis that I'm facing. It would be difficult for me to confess to an 18-year-old girl that I owe at least 1 lakh rupees. Although it may not be a large sum, for someone uncertain about their future and lacking motivation, it can feel like an overwhelming

amount of money and a tremendous burden. I can't tell you because you can't solve this problem and it might lower my image in your eyes.' I thought.

'Yes, everything will be fine,' I said.

Upon arriving home, I aimlessly wandered around. I searched for every way to pay off the debt. I was avoiding all unknown calls and messages but they were continuously calling me and sending messages with different name. There was only option left was to seek help from my friends. It wasn't hard to ask them for money. The hard part was, what would I tell them? Why would I need so much money? What was I doing in the last couple of years? I long processed it, but concluded nothing. There was no way. I was just lying in my bed suddenly her message popped.

'My father's catering firm's annual return needs to be filed; would you go with me to an income tax lawyer? You could understand him better,' she said.

'Okay, I will.' I replied.

'Even Tanu's dead father had a lot of money. He took care of two families if I believe her mother. He was filing the taxes. Look, where am I?' I thought.

If you are a dwarf with a million dollars, you discover that every tall person has far more wealth than you. You will consider every thin person to be blessed if you are overweight. Even if you are a crippled government official, every subordinate you have ever had has led you to believe that a person with a normal ability is superior to a disabled officer. I was a debt-ridden, impoverished man who saw money everywhere. Everywhere, in Tanu's father's account, in my brother's account.

We seek things we lack.

The next day, we visited the lawyer's office. After some consultation, we found that the previous tax had not been filed and a lump sum amount around seventy thousand needed to be deposited immediately. I saw vacancy board in the lawyer's office– 'Work part time 3-4 hours, should be expert in MS Excel and basic internet stuff.' I asked him if I could work part time. He said yes, but the salary was very low. The salary was an insult to me, but I took the job anyway as it was part-time.

She never imagined I could work like this.

'Never thought you would work here,' she said.

'Never thought I could go this low for work.' I said to myself.

'It's part time. Better to do something than nothing,' I said.

I started working from the next day. In one week, I learned almost everything regarding the GST returns. I told my brother and asked for money in advance. He gave me ten thousand rupees. I immediately paid one EMI to stop the spammers. But they were multiple people and bot calls. Still, I was disturbed. A month later, I got paid six thousand rupees.

And when you earn money after a long time, you literally don't want to spend it anywhere, not a single penny. Though the payment was just a pebble, but it was hard- earned. Either I wanted to save it or I want to pay all my debts from it, and that was impossible. I had to work more. And like I said, money elevates your confidence. When I had those six thousand rupees in my account, I was thinking I could go anywhere and eat whatever I wanted.

In the evening, she would come to pick me up and either we sat at the Ghats or ate something.

'That lawyer wants me to enrol in a Chartered Accountant or Company Secretary course,' I said.

'Must be in his favour,' she said.

She furrowed her eyebrows. It looked like she was completely disagreeing with me.

'Do you have any bad or weird thoughts about my work?' I asked her.

'Just be honest,' I said.

'I don't feel you belong there. You're contradicting yourself,' she said.

'I feel that too.'

'If you have to do a work or job, just join the academics where you are more capable and fit. At least where you can get a pay scale.' she said.

'But that will be 9 to 5,' I said.

'At least in 3-4 months you can waive off all of your debt. What would you get here in a year?' She hit me with words.

Her voice had changed. She sounded like my mother, scolding me and taunting me while absolutely making a right point. Working hard for less time will be more fruitful than mediocre working for years. She had a point—an absolute point. I was sitting silent, didn't figure out how to prove her wrong. She bruised my ego.

'Let's go, it's getting dark,' she said.

'Yes, we should go,' I said.

As I made my way to my room, she headed towards hers. I blew one cigarette and stood on the terrace. I was wondering about the people who are debt-free. And my mother always advised me not to borrow anything from anywhere since childhood. She believed one should eat his own namak and roti, but should not borrow curry or vegetables from anyone. And Tanu showed me I was but a distracted man, who was doing anything for money. I decided to leave this job.

I have a question for you. Who qualifies as a genuinely busy person? A man who spends his days trapped in his office, giving presentations from 9 to 5. Would you consider him to be a busy individual? It's possible that he is busy, but only for a limited period. I'm curious about a man who is always busy. A businessman? An entrepreneur? Sports man? Not a single one of them could be busy the whole time. Allow me to reveal to you the true nature of a person who is extremely busy.

A man who is wholeheartedly chasing something is always occupied. He works nonstop, 24 hours a day, 7 days a week. A man actively pursuing his goals sees the world as an opportunity to seize and achieve his objectives. He doesn't need motivation or willpower to achieve it. What keeps him going is the unease, discomfort that he will get if he doesn't meet his goal. It's his stubbornness and persistence towards his goal that keeps him going. And when a goal becomes an obsession, then the person who is willing to achieve it won't care how would he reaches it. He would reach there anyhow.

So, a busy man is one who is in a relentless pursuit of something and has made his goal his obsession.

My goal was to become debt- free at any cost. I wanted to call my friends, but I was sure that no one would give me over ten or twenty thousand, so I availed an opportunity. The firm that belonged to Tanu's father. It had to pay nearly seventy thousand. I convinced Tanu that I would pay the tax and that she should transfer the money to my account. As soon as I received the money. I promptly settled my loan. Initially, my plan was to settle my loan before moving on to paying theirs after a specific period. I had planned to settle their debt on my own. Nobody noticed because the information was only known to me. To show her and the lawyer, I generated a fake receipt.

I had turned into a dishonest person involved in both fraud and theft. Prior to this, I had done nothing illegal, but this was my first time. I could sense it showing on my face. There was a noticeable shift in my facial expression. I was filled with fear at the thought of seeing her. My face resembled that of a thief or a fraud. I told the lawyer that I won't come after next week. I needed to find another work, and I quit the job.

I gained Tanu and her family's trust entirely, and now I could visit her home randomly. At any time. Her mother, she, and I we used to have long conversations. Tanu had uplifted her skills and all of us frequently visited many places and restaurants. Some neighbours were jealous. Some people seek happiness in other people's misery. Her mother took all the burden of her father's business on her shoulders. Now she had become a busy lady. Tanu had the responsibility of her home.

Initially, I was afraid to face her, but when nothing happened and no one found anything suspicious, I became relaxed. I had in mind that I had to pay their dues before time, but I wasn't searching for the way to pay. The fatigue and the procrastination, and the mentality *'Ho jayega, dekhenge tabhi'* had put me in a more comfortable state.

And, when you have done something wrong, unethical and illegal, despite that, you don't give a shit, show no concern about this. Then, my friend, the devil has arisen inside you.

Chapter-13

The Beginning of the End

Haridwar was filled with the devotees as the great Kumbha Mela was started. They had painted every flyover and walls in the city with beautiful ancient sages and depictions. The city became a storybook. Wherever you go, you find a painting that tells something. Some pillars had the social reformers painted over them.

'They have decorated the Har Ki Pedi so marvellously.' Tanu blurted. I was sitting in their home. It was an evening time.

'Let's see it,' her grandmother said.

Tanu drove us to our destination, where we were greeted by the beautiful sight of the Ganga River reflecting the lights, shimmering like jewels on its surface. The main gate had been reconstructed, adorned with two intricately carved statues of ladies in greeting postures. As we entered the premises, we found ourselves immersed in the enchanting world of Bhole Ki Nagri. Everything around us was majestic.

To our amazement, they had constructed an iron bridge resembling Lord Ram's bow and arrow. The arrow was securely attached in the center, as if Lord Ram himself could release it at any moment. We couldn't resist capturing the breathtaking scene, and our camera shutters clicked incessantly.

Tanu's mom had thoughtfully prepared a delicious meal for us, which we enjoyed after exploring the Har ki Pedi. We sat down on the mat while her brother took a refreshing dip in the river. Tanu busily captured the picturesque moment in photographs. As we savoured the aloo poodi, the ambiance of the place seemed to enhance the flavors, making the meal even more delightful.

Amidst all this, I noticed a girl in traditional attire passing by. My eyes were drawn to her, and for a few seconds, I couldn't help but keep staring at her, captivated by her presence. 'Why are you staring at her? Is she looking pretty to you?' Tanu asked with jealousy.

I stammered.

'It's just the dress, not the girl.' I replied.

She didn't reply. I knew she was jealous.

'How could I not see her?' I thought.

It had been a while since I had aloo poori, and I was savouring every bite. It was so full of taste. We had a blast, and on our way back, we made a stop at Amrapur Ghat to enjoy some ice cream. The Ghat underwent a redesign that included the addition of a pedestrian walkway and a tiled floor. We took a few photos there and then returned to her house. Immediately, she made her way to her room and completely ignored me.

'That's not right. I just had a look at her attire.' I texted her.

'Then why do you need to explain if nothing's wrong?' She replied.

'Why am I explaining to her?' I thought.

'Because it bothered you.'

'It didn't bother me. What bothered me was your stammering. You thought before you said it. You weren't true.'

'I stammered because I didn't expect you to ask me this. No one ever asked me anything like this.'

'What on earth is this going? Why am I feeling to owe her an explanation? Is she truly…?' I thought and put my hand over my forehead.

'Mumma needs to go to Ghaziabad to claim one policy of my father's. Can we go by car?' She texted.

'Ready for the long drive?' I asked.

'You will drive. I don't have a four-wheeler license.'

'When do we plan to go?'

'As soon as possible.'

'Then tomorrow, let's ride. We will go early in the morning.'

I woke up in the early morning. I had a deep sense of unease that morning, sensing that things were not as they should be. There was a voice within me I could hear.

'Today would be a different day. Something would happen.'

That sound made me nervous. She came to pick me up. Her mother was ready, and as I observed, my hands were shivering. I didn't know the reason. We sat inside the car. She played Lord Shiva's aarti at the very first, and that was truly strengthening. I drained my fear over to lord shiva.

'May lord bless us and make this journey safe and memorable.'

Thankfully, similar to before, it was still early in the morning. Despite my complete focus on the road, I was too scared to shift the car into top gear. The vehicle was in fourth gear. I desired to maintain a constant speed, even in situations where I unintentionally applied slight pressure on the brakes, despite being aware of the potential consequences on the vehicle's fuel consumption. The first milestone was crossing Roorkee. I felt uneasy with her mother sitting with us. Each one of us was caught up in our own daydreams. I was focused on my driving and both of them were lost in their virtual cinemas. Tanu changed the song track to Punjabi.

We passed through Roorkee. I started to feel more confident in my driving skills. The more you drive a car, the better you understand it. I moved it into the fifth gear and sped up to a speed of eighty kilometres per hour. The route was straightforward and easy to understand. I quickly adapted to driving and thoroughly enjoyed the music she had on. We passed by Muzaffarnagar too.

Comfortably seated, her mother appeared at ease. She had absolute faith in me. I had been watching her in the rearview mirror. Her eyes showed a subtle sign of tiredness. She seemed pretty still. A feeling of hollowness resided within her.

'Why are you silent?' I interrupted her silence.

She abruptly looked at me, regained her senses, and chuckled a bit.

'His death is going to pay me a few lacks, maybe. Had he been alive, he would've earned a lot more?' She said and a few drops just fell off her eyes.

'Why did I ask? Why did I ask?' I scolded myself.

Tanu looked at me intensely.

'We need to look forward mamma, we will earn by ourselves.' Tanu consoled her.

'Even that's the pity, my children are growing up faster than usual. In their age of fun and activities, they are thinking about this family, they are thinking of earning. How bad is that,' she said. Tanu just dropped the volume of the song.

'You have a habit of catching and holding onto the grief until you collapse. Just let it go,' she said.

'Actually, that line should be mine, in my way.' I thought.

She spoke very well. About catching and holding the grief. In the meantime, I forgot to see that I was over speeding, 120kmph. I saw the speedometer and felt a turbulence. I slowed down to 80kmph.

An hour before our destination, we stopped at a midway break and ordered tea and snacks. I was staring at the highway from the chair. A stunning scene caught my attention. An ox was pulling a cart that a man was sitting on. He was transporting food for his livestock. Something was being played on the radio. His cart was on the left side of the road. Beside the busy highway, he was dressed in traditional garb, with a turban over his head and a modest white dhoti and kurta. The route was crowded with countless cars, trucks, and buses, and no one was willing to reduce their speed. By the time I could finish my tea, he had covered nearly 300 meters, and a hundred cars had already overtaken him. He was unaffected. Similar to my grandfather, he seemed unaffected by anything. He resembled him exactly. I felt comfortable inside. I felt the corruption inside us that has already breached our souls.

'Let's go,' I heard Tanu's voice.

Once again, the next hour-long trip was filled with complete silence. No one was willing to speak. Maybe Tanu could, but because of his mother's serious mood, she wasn't taking any chance. While my hand rested on the gearshift, I sensed a gentle tapping and noticed her silently laughing.

'So, you found a way.' I thought and chuckled.

I saw her mother; she was taking a nap.

'Play some slow music,' I said.

'Why slow? Why do you always want everything slow in your life? Back there you watched the ox cart. You should've been born 50 years ago.'

'You were watching me, watching that cart.'

'There was nothing slow than the cart on the road. I'm not sure how many stories you would have come up with while watching that cart.'

'Even I don't know that much about myself.'

'People like you cannot know yourselves. Other people get to know you.'

'You scare me sometimes. You observe me when I observe something.'

'And that could be a problem, if she could see positive inside me. She could guess the negative too, about how deep would I reach if it comes to a fraud.' I thought.

We arrived at the office at last, and an agent greeted us. We were seated in the car when her mother and he approached the claim departments.

'Do you need something? Something to eat.' I asked.

With a deep intensity, she looked directly into my eyes. I looked into her eyes, a subtle intensity reflecting in her gaze. The vacuum that separated us fuelled the excitement. It was in a flow; her heart echoed the rhythm of the unspoken desire. I moved closer, feeling a shiver down my spine as I felt the warmth of her breath. The dim interior created an atmosphere of intimacy, as if the world outside had vanished, leaving the two of us in a suspended moment.

'May I?' I asked, my voice a whisper that hung in the air, seeking permission and conveying a depth of emotion.

She nodded; her voice lost in the hush of the ambience. Time seemed to slow down as she moved closer to me. Our lips came together in a sensitive, exploratory kiss, an equilibrium of desire and connection that painted the car with the brushstrokes of a newly discovered intimacy.

As we sat inside the cocoon of metal and glass, our hands naturally gravitated towards each other, intertwining our fingers in a beautiful display of shared vulnerability. The soft and gentle hum of the radio provided a melodic backdrop for our encounter, adding an enchanting ambiance that made it feel like we were amid a picturesque scene. With each passing moment, our kiss grew deeper, causing the world to fade away, leaving behind only the lingering sound of our synchronized heartbeats. In the confined space of the car, emotions swirled, and the simplicity of that shared kiss spoke volumes about the uncharted territory of our sprouting romance.

When we finally parted, a sweet silence enveloped us. When our eyes met, there was a shared understanding that something significant and irreversible had occurred in the depths of our connection. In the hushed aftermath, the car held the secret of our first kiss, a poignant beginning to a chapter that promised the enchantment of love.

I didn't know what she was feeling, but for me it was a horrible and beautiful thing. Actually, I wasn't sure about the thing that just started between us. It was not a fling thing. I knew she meant it. She was going to start this with me, a relationship.

'I don't know what Lord Shiva wants from me.' I thought.

Her mother finished her work and then we got the chance to visit her father's ancestral village.

'Let me show you something,' she asked me to come.

Tanu took hold of my hand and dragged me in while her mother and the elders were seated inside. We broke into a tiny farm that grows organic vegetables. That was really lovely. There, almost every kind of vegetables was growing. The field of yellow mustard nearby had a scent that instantly transported me back to my village. We broke into it. We were kissing each other again and there was nobody around. This kiss was so intense that our tongues were continually entwining and twisting. Even though I had a firm hold on her, she was unwilling to break free. Our kiss was interrupted when a bee landed on my cheek and I quickly wiped it away.

'That's a bee,' I said.

She laughed. My eyes were fixed on her saucy lips that I had recently experienced.

'I have made you wet. I suppose,' I said.

'And I have made you hard. You are adjusting your pants to hide your...,' she said, and we laughed.

'How do you know I was hiding my...' I asked in a funny way.

Her mother called us for tea. She cleaned her face with water. I was just looking at her.

'Wash your face too. Your lips are glowing,' she said to me.

Chapter-14

Thing or A Fling?

I was grinning. After washing my face as well, we had tea. We finally left after her mother gave a final greeting to everyone. We both felt like we were charged up as we sat in the car. I was feeling incredibly wonderful because of a unique energy. Her face, however, was glowing in a very other way. That day, I could drive forever. Her mom remained calm.

After those two long, intense, and incredible kisses, all barriers simply vanished. I felt an overwhelming surge of masculinity. It had been quite some time since I had a partner, and I was still a virgin. I couldn't even remember the last time I had kissed someone. I was never the type of person to jump into bed with someone right away. For me, a connection was necessary — lengthy conversations, countless meetups, and plenty of kisses before I would even consider it worthwhile. It was something special, something that shouldn't be considered normal. Moreover, based on what I had studied, it was more than just a physical act. It involved an exchange of energy, a sacred atmosphere. My past relationships were always filled with intense emotions, but I had never gone further than kissing. A kiss, to me, was something that had to be earned. A genuine, heartfelt kiss is priceless. It only happened when both people had the right chemistry. Sometimes, you might have to wait years for that perfect kiss. Tanu's kiss had exactly that vibe.

While she was young and attractive, I was an ordinary 30-year-old Indian man. She had a lot of options, including dating a testosterone-fuelled male who is more physically fit and active. I was confused about why she would pick a failure like me. My shoulders were weighed down with an incredible burden now. We reached a mutual understanding and now it was my duty to tell her the truth, but I couldn't.

'I will work and pay to avoid the explanation.' I said to myself.

'What if the whole thing was a fling?' I thought.

I looked at her. She looked at me and raised her eyebrows to know what I was thinking. I smiled, and she smiled back with shyness.

'No, that won't be just a fling thing. She knew what she was doing.' I thought again.

I was driving confidently, and the journey was so full of fantasy that within no time, Roorkee came.

'Let's eat something,' Tanu said.

There was a fast-food court. We took a halt there. As her mother approached the court before us, she grabbed my hand.

'Your mother could see us.'

'That line should be mine. Girls pretend like this,' she said, and removed her hand.

'Sometimes I would like to behave like a girl, and you as a boy,' I said to her.

'So, you have plans for me? Great. You planned it in the car,' she picked on me.

'I just planned it.'

'Save it for later,' she said. We moved to a stall, and she ordered almost everything. We were hungry.

We ate momos, spring rolls, chowmeen, and pasta. She packed food to take back home.

After dropping them off, I went straight to my room. It was completely dark.

'You left so soon. You should've stayed a bit,' she texted.

'But we can't talk there, here we could talk infinitely,' I just made up the text.

'Since when were you craving for the kiss?' I asked her.

'I wanted to, but I wasn't sure earlier to step up, but you won my heart a long time ago,' she said.

'You are familiar with me. Nearly all of it. Even though I've told you a lot, I'm still a virgin. An extremely sentimental individual. Occasionally, a fragile one. I'm excellent at consoling people and offering sound counsel, but I struggled to implement these suggestions on my own,' I said.

'Did I make a mistake today? You're scaring me.'

'Don't take it otherwise. I'm telling you who I am, actually. I want to be true to you.'

'Any other thing you want to tell?'

'Yes, I've stolen seventy thousand rupees from yours.' I said to myself.

'Nothing that you don't know already.'

'I don't know, but it seems like you aren't ready for this. I thought you would be happy to take me as your girlfriend. But I'm disappointed.'

When she said this, I broke into tears. A person was ready to love me unconditionally, but I was a fool to let my fear prevent me from accepting her wholeheartedly.

'Come to me tomorrow as soon as possible,' I said.

'Don't worry, I won't hurt you,' I said further.

'You already have. Bye,' she wrote.

'I've deceived you, Tanu. It's not that you have some flaws. I am unworthy of you and I can't tell you that.' I said to myself.

Next day she came to me. Everything was normal. I experienced nausea when I locked eyes with her.

'Would you like to have some tea? Oh, shit fuck, I forgot you didn't like tea. What would you like to have?' I asked her.

'What something special you have for me?' She said, purely seductively.

'Oh, fuck it.' I murmured as I plucked her from her behind, placed her on my bed, and proceeded to suck her neck. She began to make increasingly alluring noises. With a burst of fury, I kissed her intensely and slipped my tongue into her mouth. I kept kissing her until I felt our mouths merge into one. I touched the upper region of her right breast. She stopped my progress.

'Not now,' she said.

'Okay,' I said, and we got up.

I embraced her with a hug and wrapped my arms around her. She had everything covered. I felt as though I were a giant tree. I whispered something to her, and she held onto me with even greater strength.

'I love you, Tanu. Never let me be alone.'

We were crying together and giving each other hugs. An elegant young girl of early twenty years old had captured the heart of a thirty-year-old man. A rare instance, as perceived by the majority of individuals. Then we shared another kiss. There was no harmonic imbalance; she was just fascinated with me. She could have easily fallen in love with a younger, more attractive boy, but she chose me.

The story gained momentum. Every time I went to her house, we would exchange kisses. If we happened to be outside, we would find a suitable spot to share a passionate kiss. Whenever she visited my house, we would always share kisses, and sometimes she would allow me to enjoy her beautiful, round breasts. I found comfort in resting my head on her breasts for a few minutes.

'I'm also a virgin,' she said one particular day.

'But you had relationships.'

'So did you.'

'For a boy, it's hard to get into a girl's pants, but a girl can easily ask a boy to sleep with her and he won't refuse.'

'I chose not to. I wasn't ready, and they were assholes.'

'As I previously mentioned, I never felt the need for sex immediately, and I also suffered from the fear that I wouldn't be able to do it well because I hadn't done it.'

'Everyone has their first time.'

'I wanted my first to be memorable, not pre-ejaculated or bloody or shameful.'

'You still have this phobia?'

'Not really. You want to do it?'

'Fifty-Fifty.'

'Then we won't do it.'

'I want you to make the other fifty possible.'

'That's the point. I have no experience. I want you to be ready for this. Ignoring the outcome, whether it will be bad or good.'

'Just ignore it. We will see another time.'

We were collapsing into one another's arms. Since I was the bigger guy, she was actually more into mine. I was staring at her reddened cheeks from all the smooching I had done. She was absorbed in her own world. She had my fingers in the game. My phone rang as soon as we entered our own private space. The lawyer made the call. I was sweating in no time at all. Never had I received any call so horrifying. I was positive he had discovered my theft.

'Maybe he received some notice in his e-mail.' I thought.

She noticed me.

'What happened? Why are you sweating?' She asked.

'Nothing,' I lied.

He called me again. She saw the screen.

'Why aren't you picking up his call?' She asked.

'He will ask me to come. He wanted my help, and he has been calling me from the last week. I just don't want to go,' I clarified.

'Then relax. Just silence your phone,' she said.

I silenced my phone. The lawyer just interrupted the whole ambiance, so she got up and fixed herself.

'Okay, will call you when I have time,' she said.

'Sure, love,' I said and kissed her.

I simply placed one palm on my forehead and picked up the phone as she left my room. Just before I called him, I had a thought. It was so scary. I felt like a criminal who was just going to be convicted by the court.

'If he finds me guilty, then I will accept it and search for other ways to make things right.' I thought.

I made a phone call to him.

'I'm rearranging my office. Can you come and help?' He asked.

'Of course I can, but I don't have a vehicle to come to you,' I said.

'Oh, see if you could arrange.'

'Okay, as soon as I get any bike, I will be there.'

'And share Tanu's father's firm details with me.'

'Okay, sure. I'm coming in half an hour.' My body became numb as I gave my reply. I had to reach there quickly before he could find any alternative way to open her father's account.

Chapter-15

A Million Things

I didn't have a bike. She had the option to drop me, but I had to let her go. I shared an auto and arrived at his office and sat down. Another individual was assisting him as he moved his computer from one workstation to another. I assisted him in setting everything up. My throat was drying up from the anxiety of what lay ahead. He instructed him to get me some water. For him, everything was as usual.

'Log in to their account and provide me the printouts of their taxes for the last financial year,' he said to me.

'Last financial year or the current financial year?' I asked. I knew he would catch me.

'Last financial year,' he said.

I printed them out. A few minutes later, Tanu and her mother arrived at his office. That moment was a moment of confession. Tanu saw me and stared at me. She was probably thinking, why was I there since I didn't want to? I faked my smile.

'Are you working again here?' Her mother asked.

'No, no, I came here just to help him,' I said.

She gave him the passbook that was required for the filing. To calculate the interest.

'The prior lawyer incorrectly filed the returns for the last three to four years. I must make that right. You aren't receiving the refund because of this,' he said to her.

'What should we do?' She asked.

'Just hand me the documents and I will correct it by tomorrow. I will need the OTP,' he said.

'Okay, just call us before you file,' Tanu said, and they left.

'I need to pee,' I said to him and rushed to the toilet.

Since he wasn't planning to file for the current financial year, I relieved myself there and briefly unwound. So, I had time to correct my mistake. I provided him all the details, and then I got Tanu's call.

'How did you go there?'

'Auto.'

'He called me multiple times so...' I said further.

'I'm coming. Let's eat something,' she said.

Yes, indeed. Saying that, I waited for her. When she arrived, we rode the red scooty around the streets of Jwalapur. We ate the restaurant's delicious red pasta after she introduced me to it. I knew she was picking up on my responses because I wasn't saying much. She said nothing at all. We conversed briefly while sitting on the Prem Nagar Ghat. Our journey to our homes followed. I opened my OneDrive. I was working on an unfinished book about four brothers who grew up apart and eventually cross paths in a highly dramatic setting. After finishing my first draft, I looked up publishing houses online at random.

Next day, I got a call from the publishing house.

'Sir, I'm Diksha and I'm here to assist you throughout the entire process of your book. You can ask or share anything,' a girl spoke over the phone.

'Actually, Diksha, the book is not completed yet. I just wanted to ensure whether your publishing house would approve it.'

'Our editor has read your sample pages, and he is curious. You just need the guidance of our professionals.'

'But still, the book is needs to be completed.'

'Add me on your WhatsApp and keep me updated.'

'Okay.'

A few seconds later, I got a message.

'Sir, this is Diksha, and keep me posted about your progress.'

I saw her DP. A young, pretty lady was standing beside a dog. I didn't know where it came from, but I complimented her.

'Pretty DP.'

And within a few minutes, she video-called me. Against my usual habit, I picked up a video call that day.

My intention was to confirm whether she was naturally pretty or if she had a makeup face. I was sitting in my chair. I answered her call.

'Hello sir, how are you?' She asked me.

She was quite attractive in appearance. She had her nose pierced. Her teeth were smoothly aligned. There was a tiny bindi adorning her brow. Loose strands of hair framed her face.

'Hi Diksha, I'm fine, what about you?'

'Sir, I want to be a writer too, but when I sit to write, I just can't.'

A smile came upon my face.

'You're smiling,' she said.

'Why do you want to write?' I asked her. I wanted to talk to her. She was from Raipur and her accent was catchier than her looks. It was like another dose of dopamine to me.

'I want to be an author. I want to leave my legacy in my books.'

'Have you felt heartbroken ever?' I asked.

'No. I was in a girls' hostel.'

'Ever felt happiest?'

'Daily. There is no sorrow in my life. My family is a joint family and we all live happily.'

'Do you watch movies? Any sad movie you ever watched?'

'Tere Naam.'

'When did you feel sad throughout that movie?'

'When she commits suicide. She shouldn't have died. She should have waited for him,' she said.

'So, you have an alternate ending for the movie?'

'Yes, it could be.'

'So, write it in your words.'

'Yes, I can write it.'

'If you can't think, you can't write. When you disagree with something that means you have alternatives for it. Your mind has thought about something. That something should be put in words,' I said.

'That's the easiest way you just told me to write. I disagree with many things.'

'That means you have many things to write.'

'And how could I write a whole story?'

'We will talk about this later. First, write the alternate ending for Tere Naam movie.'

'Okay, I will call you tomorrow.'

'Sure.'

She ended the call, and I came to realize something about myself. I had grown more impudent. I completely lost my integrity and sense of responsibility. My phone was resting on my stomach while I slept in bed. I didn't plan on making reparations for my mistake. Additionally, the funds I utilized for my gain were legitimate funds. It would be easy to frame me as a scammer. I wasn't taking care of my parents, nor was I attending to them. I was dishonest with the girl who had become emotionally attached to me. Despite knowing that I had already betrayed their trust, how is it possible for me to have feelings for her? The most troubling thought that came to me was: How will I ever marry her? She had only just started embracing life. I could only delay getting married for a year or two.

I had this idea in my head that I would be married before I turned thirty, even though I wasn't being forced to get married. Things were crumbling. Tanu remained silent. She didn't text or call. Later, at midnight, I felt compelled to text her because of my emotions. I sent her a text. She remained silent. After fifteen minutes, I texted her once again. She didn't respond once more. When I called her, she hung up.

Then I texted her:

'If there is something serious going on, please tell me right now.'

'I don't think things will work between us. You will be always you, and when it comes to relationship, I'm possessive but you don't want to,' she texted.

'We can work out on this tomorrow. You know me—a million things cross through my head. I just don't want to lose you,' I replied.

'I hope your words match your actions. Good night,' she wrote.

'Good night, love,' I replied.

I was certain that her Instagram was overwhelmed with message requests. My priority was to be loyal to her, and then I desired to develop feelings of love for her. Instead of seeing me as a drowsy crocodile lazing in the sun on the rock, I wanted her to see me chasing my goal. The pink lips that had momentarily propelled me into heaven. I suddenly had a strong desire for a kiss. I hoped the sun would rise soon. My eyes were too stubborn to close, so I prayed for sleep. Like someone who is thirsty and craves water, I was missing her. My heart ached to take her in my arms again. I hoped to lose her in my large embrace. I wanted to kiss her forehead. There were a couple of photos of me with her I was staring at. I zoomed in and examined every detail in her photo. I was losing my mind. I desired to visit her room. Then my brother got up from another room for the pee. I was at the peak of my hormones and he just cut the ladder.

'Why don't you sleep, lover?' He said to me.

I ignored my brother. Her face seemed to orbit around me, capturing my attention from every angle. My heart ran out of words as I attempted to compose a poem for her to pass the time, leaving it incomplete. I was in a maze of words, running back and forth. I was disappointed that I couldn't compose a poem for her. Faced with a mental block, I took a break from my laptop and reclined on my bed.

Chapter-16

Generation Gap

Next morning as I woke up it was 8 am. I checked my phone. Her message was there.

'Coming at 9 am.'

I got up and fixed myself, completed my morning chores, and took a bath. It became my habit that before she could arrive; I imagined it. So, when I found that my heart had this turbulence, I knew she had come or was about to come. I could foresee her.

As she came, I was sipping tea and eating leftover food from the night.

'You didn't prepare breakfast?' She asked.

'I was not in the mood to prepare something.'

'Should I help? Do you have eggs or something?' She asked.

'I'm done. Come.'

Both of us, filled with anxiety, sat down together on my bed. A specific incident was expected to occur. Before I could utter a single word, she approached me and planted a kiss on my lips. As we continued to kiss passionately, we slowly began to undress ourselves, revealing our bodies to one another. I leaned in and planted a passionate kiss on her, starting from her head all the way down to her toes. I had the pleasure of playing with and licking on her stunning, perfectly round breasts. I carefully and softly landed on top of her. She had become drenched all over. She emitted a joyful sound with her mouth.

Her hand was tightly grasping my fully erect manhood.

'Both of us are virgins. Are you sure you want to do it?' I whispered in her ear.

'Just do it,' she said and released her grip.

I was about to do it but again, I asked her.

'Are you sure?'

'Why are you ruining it?'

As I tried to do it, she groaned and pushed me.

'It's hurting.'

'For me, too.'

'Try once more.'

I had one virgin pornographic movie in mind. He approaches the girl cautiously at first, trapping her in a discussion before abruptly pushing quickly and obligingly. She was already moaning in pain when I inserted, and she cried out when I pushed.

'Pull it out.'

I pulled out.

'It's painful. I won't do it.'

'Indeed, it was. Leave it. Just lay with me.'

She was nestled in my arms.

'My kitty.'

'My grizzly bear.'

'Grizzly bear?' I exclaimed.

'Have you seen yourself? Hairs and hairs are all around.'

'Genetics.'

'Even if you get hair loss, you have plenty of them for transplant.'

'My ancestors blessed me with these plenty of hairs.'

'I didn't feel shy when you undressed me. I felt like you have already seen me multiple times.'

'I feel shy because of hairs.'

'Now you don't need to, my grizzly bear.'

I gently touched her breasts, and once again, our lips came together. She came upon me.

'That would be more painful if you're going to try like this.'

'I'm not trying. A bird wants shelter in the eagle's paws.'

'I'm too big for you.'

'Majority of girls want big guys.'

'No one knows what a girl really wants.'

'Means?' she asked doubtfully.

'You can't tell your friends about us. They could gossip or mock us. They would say that we don't have an age gap, we have a generation gap. You would need guts to introduce me to your friends and family. Your mother knows me as your instructor, helper, and a nice guy. Not someone who could love her daughter,' I said.

'Can you introduce me to your friends?' She asked.

'My brother knows, and if I tell my friends, they would be happier than happy.'

'And why is that?'

'Since I am thirty years old and you have just reached adulthood, you are quite beautiful and attractive. They would consider it as if I've won the lottery.'

'One day, my buddies will also think that. I'm certain you would accomplish all of your goals. They will be pleased that I also won the lottery.'

'Even my family doesn't have this faith in me. They want me to do a job, get married, be a father and spend my life like ninety-five percent of the people on this earth do. I don't want to jump like a frog. I'm preparing myself for a long jump.'

'You will do it someday, I know.'

'If you're willing to give it another shot, feel free to do so. I want to end this pain once and for all,' she said further.

'No, we will take it gradually, no hurry,' I said.

We stood up, and I let her sit on my lap, where she placed her head on my chest and seized my arms. It was a remarkable moment. I was kissing her cheeks all the time.

'I should go now. Mum will get angry.'

'As you wish.'

She departed, and I felt bad. The emotion was one of extreme disgust, and it appeared as though the angel was sitting in a depressed mood over my right while the devil was grinning over the left shoulder.

'What if I tell her the truth? Would she still love me?' I thought.

'No, she would feel bad, betrayed and played by me. She might objectify herself.' I thought.

On every scale that day, I wanted to make things right. I needed to fix things urgently. Now was the time to seek help from my buddies. I visited the lawyer's office. It was a casual visit to ensure if anything was on his mind. I didn't find any. It was the month of April, and the second wave of coronavirus had hit the country so fiercely. Diksha, on the other hand sent me the alternate ending of the movie.

I read it. She wanted Nirjara, i.e., Bhumika, to get married to another guy, and later that guy would arrange for her marriage to Radhe, i.e., Salman Khan.

'That's a decent ending, but why do you want to save Nirjara?' I texted Diksha.

'That's not a happy ending. I don't want her to die,' she replied.

'Anyone can die. Anyone can be left alone. The ending you wrote would not hit the public as the original did. That's why the film was hit. She couldn't bear to be tied to another person other than Radhe. That's why she chose to die. For her, marriage wasn't a game. She wanted to be a fully committed woman to her husband,' I texted.

'You're just exceptional. Can we talk over the phone?' She replied.

'Sure.'

While we were engaged in a conversation about the movie's alternate ending, I managed to convince her I was right. Throughout the entire time, she was laughing as if I were a stand-up comedian delivering my lines from a script.

After the call, I complimented her.

'But you wrote something on your own. That's good.'

'Are you single?'

'Why are you asking this?'

'Next month I am coming to Delhi. Would you like to meet?'

'No, I won't. I don't leave my room without a purpose.'

'I have given you the purpose. I hope one day we could meet.'

'Who knows? Okay bye, talk to you later,' I said and ended the call.

As soon as I put my phone away, I started missing Tanu. I had a lot of drowsy desires after what had just transpired between us. I wanted to touch her, anywhere, at any time. My desire to undress her arose once more. Her complete expression was focused on me. She called me while I was in a fantasy land.

'I was missing you desperately,' I said before she could say anything.

'But you didn't call.'

'Actually, I was enjoying missing you. You were virtually around me. I was in my fantasy world.'

'Why were you in your fantasy world when you could've called me or met me?'

'I was about to call you. And in my fantasy, we were making love. I was undressing you. We were in our private space.'

'Actually, same here. I want to come to you. My grizzly bear.'

'Who's stopping you? Come into my arms, my Senorita.'

'You named me Senorita?'

'Don't you like it?'

'I loved it.'

'I desperately want to be there. But its evening, and I can't come,' she said and showed her constraints.

'You can come to me tomorrow at 11 am. Mum and brother would go to the market,' she said further.

The intense longing to kiss her compelled me to visit her immediately. But I had to wait for tomorrow.

Chapter-17

The Goodbye

As soon as I arrived at her place, I wasted no time and immediately began kissing her the moment I had my hands on her. Both of us were engaged in an intense battle, struggling to catch our breaths. I wanted to get inside her more and more, so I kissed her more deeply. There were moments when I thought I was kissing myself while I was kissing her. The vibe that I received was that we were in sync and connected as one.

'Should we try one more time?' she expressed her desire.

'If you wish to.'

She swiftly undressed while I matched her pace. Gently, I lifted her and settled her into bed. Shedding my own clothes, I wasted no time slipping a finger inside her. She was prepared and bathed. The aroma of her body only heightened my desire to be with her. Taking a deep breath, I savoured her scent, committing it to memory. I studied her face, sensing a mix of anticipation and trepidation. Slowly, I entered her, eliciting a pained moan, yet this time she held back from pushing me away. With her eyes tightly shut, I patiently awaited any indication from her. And then she signalled her consent, giving me the green light to continue.

'Do it.'

We were slowly doing it. Both of us were doing it properly first time. Her seductive voice was only raising my testosterone.

'How could something be so good?' She said in her pleasurable moment. Her eyes squeezed shut.

And it was really superb. I quickened my pace a little, and her delightful sound filled the entire room. She bit her lip and shifted her neck back and forth, as if she were in another reality. Her warm breath was touching my face as I stood just above her. I hesitated for a moment. When I paused, she opened her eyes to see why. I lifted her up a little and kissed her on the lips as she looked to face me.

'I wanted to lick you everywhere.'

'Do what you want, just don't stop.'

I kissed her and licked her whole body. She was fully submitted to me. The whole of me was loving the whole of her.

When we had finally completed it wonderfully, she was lying in my arms. I decided to never let go of her at that very moment. Now that my romantic life was in order, I had to make plans for our future. She offered me hope, which I thought was really lovely. And hope was a pretty

Chapter-17

The Goodbye

As soon as I arrived at her place, I wasted no time and immediately began kissing her the moment I had my hands on her. Both of us were engaged in an intense battle, struggling to catch our breaths. I wanted to get inside her more and more, so I kissed her more deeply. There were moments when I thought I was kissing myself while I was kissing her. The vibe that I received was that we were in sync and connected as one.

'Should we try one more time?' she expressed her desire.

'If you wish to.'

She swiftly undressed while I matched her pace. Gently, I lifted her and settled her into bed. Shedding my own clothes, I wasted no time slipping a finger inside her. She was prepared and bathed. The aroma of her body only heightened my desire to be with her. Taking a deep breath, I savoured her scent, committing it to memory. I studied her face, sensing a mix of anticipation and trepidation. Slowly, I entered her, eliciting a pained moan, yet this time she held back from pushing me away. With her eyes tightly shut, I patiently awaited any indication from her. And then she signalled her consent, giving me the green light to continue.

'Do it.'

We were slowly doing it. Both of us were doing it properly first time. Her seductive voice was only raising my testosterone.

'How could something be so good?' She said in her pleasurable moment. Her eyes squeezed shut.

And it was really superb. I quickened my pace a little, and her delightful sound filled the entire room. She bit her lip and shifted her neck back and forth, as if she were in another reality. Her warm breath was touching my face as I stood just above her. I hesitated for a moment. When I paused, she opened her eyes to see why. I lifted her up a little and kissed her on the lips as she looked to face me.

'I wanted to lick you everywhere.'

'Do what you want, just don't stop.'

I kissed her and licked her whole body. She was fully submitted to me. The whole of me was loving the whole of her.

When we had finally completed it wonderfully, she was lying in my arms. I decided to never let go of her at that very moment. Now that my romantic life was in order, I had to make plans for our future. She offered me hope, which I thought was really lovely. And hope was a pretty remarkable thing to me—possibly the only thing I could have wished at that time.

My phone was lying beside me. I didn't know what came into her mind, but she opened it. Then opened WhatsApp. Though I found it odd, I didn't stop her. She opened the gallery and saw the photos. Some photos were of us, too. I had some weird feeling inside because I feared whether she might find anything related to a lawyer or their tax file. But no, she found out about the chat between Diksha and me. Her face paled. She saw the video call list and found her name there, and also on my recent call list.

'When do you plan to go to Delhi or Raipur?' She asked, tears in her eyes.

'Why would I go there? Don't take it wrong.'

'She video-called you for about fifteen minutes and called you for like hours.'

'She was an over-enthusiastic girl, wanting to be a writer, so I was giving her tips.'

'She was flirting with you and then asked you to meet up, inquiring about your relationship status. She wanted to hear stories from you while you fuck her nearby the Qutub Minar or Gateway of India.'

'At the very first, it was absolutely nothing. Just block the number. Second, The Gateway of India, is in Mumbai.'

'Stop being a tutor here. I know how it works, and she is interested in you.'

'Then why didn't I delete that chat?'

'I don't know. Maybe you forgot.'

'Yes, because that's me. Random things happen to me. Still, I'm figuring out how to take care of you since I've fallen for you. However, my mind is filled with countless thoughts. I didn't expect that from you,' I said. Disappointed.

'It seems like I'm a burden to you. I'm not asking you to do anything for me.'

'Just don't do that, Tanu. You love me, then just love me. Don't possess me, otherwise bad things will happen. It's all about trust.'

'We should be like we were before. It seems like I've made a mistake. I have put you under something I shouldn't.'

'But I always wanted to kiss you. You tempted me.'

'If you're true, then you don't need an explanation.'

'Just come here.' I asked her to come into my arms.

Finally, she came. We hugged.

'That was the India Gate. Just slipped my tongue,' she said.

I laughed out loud.

'India Gate is in a wide-open area for the public to enjoy. It's not a place to fuck someone. It's a war memorial and sacred place for each Indian. You speak anything.'

Finally, she laughed too.

'I've deceived you financially, but I won't deceive you emotionally ever.' I said to myself.

Not because I didn't want to love her, but because I was afraid of loving her. It was clear why. A lie served as the foundation of our relationship. If she had been my age, perhaps she wouldn't have chosen me. A female who is already in her thirties has already become a mature, strict adult. She wouldn't pick someone who only has an ambition without a strategy for achieving it. A thirty-something who is penniless will not be chosen by her. Tanu was nineteen, and her hormones were at their highest.

And so, I went to my room. I had to do all the steps to fix this. For me, calling my pals was the only way to put things right. That was the pinnacle of the second wave. We weren't very interested in the news, so we didn't give it much thought, but Google kept bringing up daily alerts on my screen, telling me that the globe was experiencing more extreme events than I had in my life. I gave my friend Aakash, who was in Delhi, a call. During our conversation, he revealed to me he had been in a separate room with Covid for three days, subsisting on potatoes and eggs. He could not return home. I comforted him and hoped for improved health for him.

Then I called my father, and I came to know that my parents were seriously ill. The Covid had hit the village. Half of the village was infected. That news just blew me. Although they had their personal Ayurvedic doctor, who was treating them, but what I had in my mind was that what if I lost them? My father's voice was shivering and mother was speaking in the background. She was telling me to take care of my health. They refused to let me come home. Tears welled in my eyes. I froze in my bed.

Next day she called me to her home. I told her about my parents.

'You should go to your home,' she said.

'They told me not to come.'

'That's why you should go. Just understand what I'm trying to say,' she insisted.

I knew what she was implying. She knew the loss of losing a parent.

I went to the Jwalapur market with her mother. We bought apples and other stuff. Watching those red apples made me think my parents would also need them. Who would go to the market to buy for them? They needed me. The place was crowded, and no one seemed to worry about this fucking Covid. But every second my mother's and my father's face were revolving around me. It was like a spell of death seizing my heart. As we returned from the market, the TV was on. News showed that the hospitals were full, and there were not enough oxygen cylinders for the patients. People were dying like I read in history books when the plague spread. There were corpses everywhere. The worst thing was that no one could go to the dead. The dead bodies were buried or burned without the presence of their families to avoid the further spread. The pandemic had become the worst. I chose to go to my home. I asked Tanu to give me a ride to my room and told her I'd be back once my parents were okay.

She drove her scooty, and we were in my room. She hugged me. Before she could go, we made love one more time. I observed my heart was beating faster than before, and my neck was sweaty.

'You're gasping,' she said.

'Nothing, maybe we enjoyed it more today,' I said, and she grinned.

'Just come back soon. This is the first time I will be really alone.'

'We will talk over the phone. Don't worry, babe.'

'You will come back, naa?' She grabbed my hand. Placing my hands on hers, I felt a connection.

'I dream of a future where you become the mother of our daughter, who will inherit your beautiful nose.'

I spoke with a tone of assurance.

'What if I bear you a son?' She asked shyly.

'I will pray for a daughter. I'm tired of living among males,' I said.

'Let's see what plan God has for us.'

I gave her a long kiss.

'I wish we could go together,' I said.

'Maybe one day, for sure.'

'What if your mother rejects me?'

'No, my mother would not reject a person if she knows he would keep her daughter safe and sound and treat her well.'

'That's a point.'

I said my goodbyes to her, acknowledging that life unfolds like a book, with each phase representing a chapter. However, the tricky part is that it's not always clear when one chapter concludes and a new one begins. Some chapters provide clues of their impending end, while others simply come to an abrupt close, sometimes even right from the beginning or in the middle. We are often unaware of these shifts, but all we can do is adapt and handle them. At this point, everything began to change.

I glanced at her red scooty. It appeared like a slow-motion video. She adjusted her hair and hopped on the scooty, like always, without a helmet. She folded the side stand, pressed the brakes and ignited the scooty. She glanced at me, waved with her left hand, and gradually sped up. I was watching her leave me. When I entered my room, I realized I was panting and suddenly felt extremely tired. Ignoring that, I packed my bag and left for my village. During the lockdown last year, all transportation had come to a halt, and I had feared of not being able to reach my destination if buses stopped running. Finally, after a long wait, I was able to catch my bus. It was the last week of April, with summer just around the corner. As I sat at the window seat, the wind felt like December's. I understood that the virus had infected me. I maintained regular communication with Tanu. She became terrified when she knew about my health conditions. I was concerned because we had had sex a few hours ago, and I worried about the possibility of her getting infected as well. On the contrary, she was feeling fine.

Chapter-18

The Numb Heart

At last, I made it to my village, and by that time, I was suffering from a high fever. When I stood up and placed my feet on the floor, I realized I lacked the energy to take another step. I waited for a few minutes and signalled for an e-rickshaw driver. He stood there as the sole courageous person. There was nobody else present. He not only took my belongings but also escorted me to my home. I saw no one there except my mom and dad. I returned home after a long time, but I wasn't greeted with any welcome. Both of them were in terrible conditions. There were many bottles of potions placed near the khaat. I gently touched their feet, and my mother opened her eyes.

'Why have you come? I told you not to,' she said. Her voice was broken.

'I'm burning with fever, maa. I am already infected,' I said.

My father woke up. He had some strength remaining. So, he gave me warm water and provided a powder medicine.

'Take it and lie down inside,' he said.

While he was talking, I observed that the gap between his teeth had become wider and the edges of his teeth were chipped. It was a painful experience because the person who was once your source of strength needed support, and you could not provide it. Instead of doing something for them, I also became a burden. He phoned the doctor who was taking care of them.

The doctor came and inspected me. He checked my pulse.

'You need to be strong and patient. This is not a regular fever that could go in hours. It could take days or weeks. You need to be strong by mind, like your parents. Now they are healing. Their fever has gone,' he said and poured a few drops of another potion inside my mouth. Within a few minutes, I fell asleep.

It was good to hear that they were healing. I found a sense of relaxation in me. When I woke up, my cousin came into my room. I told him not to come near me.

'I've attained victory over this fever last week. Now I'm immune,' he said.

While laughing, I experienced discomfort in my facial muscles. I noticed that my cheeks had become extremely stiff. I lacked the strength to sit or even go to the restroom. I realized I had a multitude of notifications on my phone. The display was hazy. It was hard for me to concentrate on the screen because of my weak eyes. I could only see the name that appeared following the heart symbol. I was aware of whose alerts they were. Tanu's name brought me comfort. I unlocked my phone. It was so bright that I could not see. I attempted to concentrate on my phone. I went through one of the messages she sent.

'You've ghosted me.'

I called her. She immediately picked up her phone.

'You said that you would call me! It's been one day and no information,' she said.

'What?! One day?! I've been sleeping since yesterday. I thought it was a few hours ago,' I said.

'You're lying.'

'Tanu, I can't explain or convince you right now. I'm having trouble seeing my phone clearly. I am experiencing issues with my eyesight. My body is immobile. I cannot sit. Corona took me badly. I'm getting tired even as I speak to you. There's a sensation of heaviness on my chest, like I'm carrying a heavy stone. I'm constantly gasping,' I said.

The sound of crying reached my ears. I lacked the energy to comfort her. I could easily picture her in tears.

'Just stand firm with me. I'm happy that you didn't get infected. It was…one of my happiest moments when… I was with you.' I said, and the phone slipped from my palm. I could hear her saying 'hello, hello, are you there?' but my hands felt so heavy and tired that I couldn't pick the phone. My heart was racing, and I was struggling to catch my breath. I was laying in the bed. My cousin provided me with a soup. He helped me to sit in the chair.

As I sipped the soup, a moment later, I sensed my bladder was advising me to take a piss. It was good to know that one organ was working properly.

The washroom was outside. I summoned all my muscles, urging them to gather and harness their energy. It took me ten minutes to cover fifty steps to go to the washroom. Urinating felt like a hot kettle pouring dark coffee into the toilet bowl. I was wondering about the melting point of the bladder of humans. It felt like my manhood had been drenched in a chili sauce. It was extremely painful. And I was tired again. Returning was incredibly difficult, and I didn't even have the strength to cry out for help. I put my palm on the wall. My heart was about to explode. I had a feeling that I was about to fall to the ground. But again, I mustered up my courage, called my muscles not to give up, and put my foot outside the washroom. I extended my other foot forward, and after a few steps I didn't count, my foot turned awkwardly, causing me to lose balance and fall onto the ground, hitting my chest against the floor. When a person weighing ninety kilograms falls to the ground, it creates an impact. Upon hearing me, my mother promptly directed my cousin to come and pick me up.

'You should've called me,' he said.

I was trying to laugh because I didn't feel any injury. It seemed like my upper body was paralyzed. He put me back in my bed and gave me another liquid. My hope to live suddenly faded. I heard that if someone becomes paralyzed because of COVID-19, their chances of survival are extremely low.

'God, at least give me a chance to repay my debt. What would she think of me if I passed away like that?' I was swearing at God.

I desperately wanted to live. The thought of her cursing me for the rest of her days haunted me, making me regret what I had done to her.

'Even prisoners get to live the whole life in jail. What possibly had I done that wrong? 70k fraud?' I thought.

My eyelids were heavy. I was awake, but my eyes were closed. I was thinking about my brother. He was alone there, but at least he wasn't infected. Without pause, he kept calling my mother, wanting updates on everyone. He was going to work three days a week. I was still wondering why he was doing it. There was so much danger was there outside. He should've stayed home.

Once more, I was fast asleep. My father shook me in the middle of the night, waking me. I noticed him seated next to me. It gave me a glimmer of optimism that my parents were doing well. However, the price they paid was excessive. All they contained was consumed by their bodies. Cheeks were loosened. Their faces became pale. And there was almost no strength in them. I had to take care of them somehow. I could not respond to my father's attempts to communicate with me. All I could do was observe him speak. When my senses returned a few seconds later, I heard him advise me to eat before taking the medication.

'I couldn't sit. My hands are not responding, nor is my back,' I said.

My cousin was called, and he helped me to sit. I sipped that green soup. Completely tasteless and odourless. Then again, I lay down in my bed. In the last week of April, I was wrapped in a thick blanket. I checked my phone. I saw hundreds of missed calls and video calls notifications. The screen was too bright and was bothering me, so I put my phone back.

The next morning, I woke up at 6 am. I felt some kind of volcanic activities inside my stomach. I called my mother. She came to me. I grabbed her hand and rushed to the washroom. I vomited. My body rejected everything that was supposed to be digested by now. I returned to my bed and cried. I was assuming that my days were over in this world.

'Take me to the hospital,' I told my parents.

When I mentioned the hospital, my mother started crying too. My father came and he told me to hold on to the situation. He told me about the conditions of the hospitals, but I was insisting. My mother called our doctor, and he came instantly.

'That's good if he vomited. His fever will be gone by evening,' he said to my mother. I was listening to him.

He poured a few drops of medicine into my mouth. When he was gone, the whole family gathered in our living room—both of my uncles, aunts, and cousins.

'Find a girl and get him married. Fulfil your duties as a parent before something happens to anyone of you,' Tau ji was saying to my parents about me.

I, on the other hand, was thinking about how optimistic they were. I was going to die, and they were thinking of getting me married.

'This fever left nothing inside me. I had pain in my knees and I wasn't expecting much life ahead,' my father's voice crumbled.

'Your boy is a graduate. Put him to some work and get him married. I have some suggestions,' Tau ji said further.

'Let him be fine. We will talk later,' my father said.

As their conversation ended and they moved from there, I had another trauma inside my head. Of course, it was about marriage.

All of a sudden, an immense pain gripped my chest, and my legs began to shake uncontrollably. I was experiencing pain in my knee, but fortunately, my fever had subsided. The blanket, due to the intense heat, transformed into a scorching oven. I was not burning anymore, but my whole body was in tremendous pain. The chest pain, I recalled, resulted from the injury that I sustained when I fell. The pain that I felt during my childhood Kabaddi accident was identical to the pain I just experienced. Because of the medications I took and the fact that I had a high fever, I didn't feel any pain. At precisely 3 pm, I found myself watching everything with greater precision, and to my relief, the brightness of the phone was no longer causing me a headache.

I was healing. Experiencing comfort, I was relieved that my body fought off this terrible fever. I resurrected finally.

I called Tanu.

'How is it going there?' I asked.

'Why did you do that?' She asked.

I realized she had caught my fraud.

'I was about to make things right. Then this corona happened,' I said.

'You could've told me. Come here immediately; otherwise, we will take legal action. I will sue you and make sure that you would spend the rest of your life in jail for what you have done to me and to us,' she said.

'To you? What do you mean to you?' I asked.

'Your brother told me everything. I know that you're getting married,' she said.

'My brother didn't like you. He might have said this. Ignore him.'

'I can't trust you anymore. I always had this issue. You made me right.'

'I will be there the day after tomorrow.' I said, hanging up the call.

My fever had gone, but still I was gasping. I was on the terrace and sitting in my chair. I dialled one of my friends' numbers.

'Listen Ashu, I have an emergency and I need 70k by tomorrow,' I said.

He was a government servant. I knew if someone could help me quick, it would be him.

'I had invested my money. I only live on half of my salary.'

'Just do something bro, I will repay you in instalments.'

'All I can do is to give you whole of my salary of this month.'

Luckily, it was April's last day, and he was about to get his salary by tomorrow.

'It would be great if you do it,' I said.

'How would I spend the next month, bro?' He asked.

'I will arrange some money for your basic expense by the 10th of May.'

'But what's that emergency? Is everything okay at home? Your parents?'

'We've been resurrected from death. Thanks to corona.'

'Oh, take care bro, people are dying like street dogs nowadays.'

'Yeah, okay, I will talk to you later. Ping me when you transfer the money.'

'Okay.'

I packed my bags again. My clothes were dirty. I told my parents that I had an interview and I needed to go. They insisted me not to go, but I had decided. The next day, my friend transferred the money.

'I should've borrowed from him earlier.' I thought, cursing myself.

After taking the medicine, I caught the bus. I directly headed to the lawyer. He messaged me to meet there. I entered his office.

'I never expected this from you. We would never know if Tanu hadn't cross-checked the transfer details.' The lawyer said, and I came to know that it was Tanu who caught me and not the lawyer.

Tanu and her mother were sitting in the chair. They ignored me like I was their profound enemy. Their ignorance made me believe everything was over with them because none of them asked me about my health. I was still on medication. My body needed the rest. My chest was aching.

I bought a glucose and soft drink hoping if any of them wanted to drink or make a conversation. No one gave a shit. I was sitting silently, and the lawyer was analysing the amount.

'Do you have the money in your account right now? Then I will proceed,' he said.

'Yes, make all of this right, right now,' I said.

'If you had the money, then why did you do it?' he said.

'I'm not in a state to tell you anything. My body is collapsing,' I said.

Her mother looked at my face. Her face was like she wanted to cry, like she wanted to ask why I did this, but Tanu held her back. And she knew I was sick. My brother was calling me repeatedly. I was constantly ignoring his call.

I provided the lawyer my net banking details, and within an hour, he filed all the taxes that were remaining because of my mistake.

'Everything has been resolved. I'll email the information to you,' he said as they exited after he briefed them.

'At least you could've told me,' the lawyer said to me.

'This corona made everything messy.' I said and exited his office, too. My eyes were igniting fire. Everything was so shiny and blurry. I managed to reach to my brother's room somehow and lay down on the bed. I never put that much strength into any work that I put it there.

'You should've consulted with me first before telling your mother,' I texted Tanu.

'You played with me and my mother. For the first two days, I prayed for you to get well soon, but as soon as

I found out that you're getting married and you deceived us, I wanted you to die,' she texted.

'I was going to tell you. I said nothing about my marriage. You never trusted me.' I replied.

'You had sex with me. You robbed me of my dignity. You took advantage of my vulnerable widowed mother and us. She remained silent upon discovering the truth. You asshole, filthy bastard, I curse you to rot in a hell. If my father were still alive, I can assure you that you would spend the rest of your life in prison,' she said.

I was reading this text. The tears were rolling out of my eyes, and I saw her profile picture vanishing. She blocked me.

I had felt this before—the improper closure in a relationship. I came here to correct my mistake and to discuss the further planning with her. I got up and went to my brother.

'Why did you lie to her about my marriage?' I asked vigorously.

'That's not the time for stupidity. Because of her, you were more distracted. I did what was needed to be done,' he explained.

If I had possessed enough strength in my arms on that day, I would have undoubtedly beaten him until he begged for his life. I would've shot him if I had the gun. Rage coursed through me, but I lacked the vigour of youth, feeling as feeble as an old man. I took a seat and placed my hand on my forehead.

'She's in love with me,' I said.

'She is a young girl. She will find another fool soon,' he said.

'How could this end in such a way? Within five days? It can't be. Just unimaginable. Unbelievable. How could? How could she do this to me? She would've slapped me, abused me. Instead, she left me. That was her love?' I was constantly fighting within myself.

'How could she?'

Chapter-19

Social Acceptance

Next morning, I woke up and suddenly I realized there was nothing left in Haridwar without her. The whole town was black and white. Every road, every place had a memory of her red scooty and us.

'What would I do without her in this city?'

I departed back to my village. My parents were worried. I didn't change my clothes, nor did I eat anything. I lay down on the bed, and my tired eyes just shut off.

The following morning, I looked at my phone. Not a reply. I had a sneaking suspicion that my brother had said something awful and profound to her, but she still needed to tell me, at least. There was no heartache or a miserable feeling like a breakup. I felt shaky. I used to have an odd habit of foretelling the plot of movies and web series, and most of the time, especially in Bollywood, my predictions came true. It was like someone close to me was murdered, and instead of mourning, I was only thinking about the killer. It was like a tragedy, like a movie, and during the four days I spent battling death, I did not know what would happen. It was more than my gut feeling. That was no way for a girl like Tanu to conclude a relationship.

Conversely, one of my relatives was searching for a suitable career for me, and my parents were on the lookout for a bride. I had no questions from anyone. They were deeply afraid of the pandemic. Their main thought was to finish their responsibilities before they succumbed to death.

'No matter how good I make this tea, everything is tasteless. I can only feel either salt or sugar. No flavour, no jaayka,' Mother was saying to Father while serving the tea.

Suddenly Chacha ji came. Chacha ji was someone in my life who held as much importance to me as my father. I always loved him as he always blessed me and never said a thing to me. He came to me and sat in the chair.

'What about your interview?' He asked politely.

'Can't say anything,' I replied.

'You've grown enough now. Take a peek at your parents. They are afraid. I want you to assume full responsibility for this house. Offer peace to your parents. Your brother is likewise concerned about you because you've already taken your time. There are some good matches for you because of your father's reputation. Just choose the girl, and we'll proceed on. There should be no delay,' he said to me.

If this discussion had come from my father or mother, I would've strictly refused. Chacha ji put me in a dilemma. He patted my hand. I approved nothing, but I nodded my head. I didn't want to disapprove anything he said. And logically, he was right, and now I was almost agreeing to what he said.

It was the time to accept the reality. The time to bury these shitty, unresolved heart matters. But my heart was numb and lost—almost dead. She left me in a maze. It was unacceptable for me to move on like that. I deserved an explanation. Then I recalled the memory of the lawyer's office. I was no one to them. It was like they didn't know me.

'Maybe that suffering could bring peace for me someday.' I thought.

I was angry, guilty, and disappointed.

'Maybe she wants me to text her?' I thought.

'I had such a high fever that I narrowly escaped death, but it made no difference to her and her mother. Despite being in a feeble condition, I was compelled to go to the office. This work could have been postponed for a few days. When they had nobody, they didn't even consider the fact that I was there. She threatened me with police and legal action. Do I really deserve everything that has happened to me? Haven't I done anything deserving of a little respect from them?' My expressions changed to one of anger as I thought about this.

'Mamma, I want to get married,' I said to Mother.

My mother made a strange face at me. She could assume that I intended to settle down and had given up on my fantasy world. 'You need to take a job first,' she said, after a deep thought.

I was not thinking clearly. I felt like an alcoholic all the time—the consequences of that damn corona. When I woke up the following day, I discovered hundreds of hairs clinging to my pillow. I ran my fingers through my hair, and when I glanced at my palm, it was filled with strands of hair. I was filled with fear.

'I am going to be bald. Just look at the pillow.' I grabbed my mother's hand, and she saw this. She immediately called the doctor.

'This is the aftereffect of the fever and don't worry, the hair will grow back,' he said to me.

My worries were more about the things that were going on in my life than I was about losing hair. I discovered that everything in life was utterly unjust. The more carefree I tried to be, the more unfair things kept happening to me.

That evening, I met my village friend who happened to be a senior in my school and was running a coaching institute. Before I could ask or say anything to him, he offered me a job.

'Would you like to teach Computer Science to our 11th and 12th students?'

I chuckled.

'I will pay you a decent amount,' he said further.

'Problem is not the payment. Actually, I cannot give any assurance how long I will be able to teach,' I said.

'But I have a solution. I will design 45 days of Python, C and C++ language video course. We will sell the course, and I will be available twice or thrice a week for problem- solving. We will sell it for 3000,' I said further.

'And my share?'

'1000. If 30 students take this course, you will instantly earn 30k within a day.'

'How much time would you take to prepare this course?'

'I will record three lectures daily and you will show them according to your timetable. If any query persists, I will be there after the class.'

'Why don't you come here and teach?'

'In case I got shifted from here. I could still record the lectures from anywhere, and you could use these videos in as many lectures as you want. We just need a camera and a microphone. I had a whiteboard at my home,' I said.

The deal was done. I informed my mother about it, and she found the idea quite creative. The concept was actually new to the village. I got the room and organized it. Both my cousin and I have devoted ourselves to this job. His work was to assist me. With no breaks, I managed to record five lectures on the very first day. Despite the turmoil in my heart, I remained committed to fulfilling my promise.

I wanted to accept this new reality. I was engaging in actions that would help me become a person who was socially accepted and well-liked by others. No one disturbed me. I didn't care to look at my phone or to check my messages or calls. I removed all the OTT apps and avoided all fresh content. Money and social acceptance were the new motivation. This time I was acting on a gut feeling. I sent him the videos I had recorded. He approved my content. I then became embroiled in that stuff. The hair was still falling out, but I disregarded it all. I created my schedule. Get up early, work, have breakfast, do morning chores, and go for a walk.

I got my share from him. Initially, I settled my debt with Ashu.

The hard part was the night. I had become scared while lying in bed at night. I used to love being alone at night, but something had changed. The day was serene, filled with hustle and activity. The village was always bustling with people and their amusing news. But after 9 pm, the village became haunted to me. There were no streetlights. I started hating the night. Even when I walked in the evening, I couldn't get tired enough to sleep. My night's sleep was gone. I tried shaking my legs rapidly, but my brain felt too awake. I felt terror in my heart. Her memory haunted me—her scooty, her car, her mother, and Haridwar. It became traumatic, but I couldn't tell anyone.

The following evening, I brought a bottle of whiskey with me. When I climbed into bed, I poured myself a large glass and drank it all in one go. I had an urge to sleep, even though it felt like my throat was on fire. I sighed in agony from a stomachache after about thirty minutes. Upon hearing my loud cries, my father quickly arrived and immediately called the doctor. I was in my bed, rolling over—from one corner to the next. I ingested the potion that was prescribed by the doctor. I was throwing out the entire meal and the whisky.

'Did you drink?' The doctor asked me, whispering in my ear.

I nodded my head affirmatively.

'You should know that you're still healing. Your liver is weak, you're weak. Never do this again,' he scolded me.

'I can't sleep.'

Then he gave me some pills.

'These will help you. But one at a time. First, try to sleep without them. Don't make them your habit.'

I took one pill on my tongue after he left, and it disappeared in five seconds along with the saliva. Additionally, I understood from body science that it would properly mix into my blood only after at least ten to twenty minutes. Thirty minutes passed and nothing occurred. The silence while I lay in bed scared me. My arms and legs were twitching. My heart was racing so quickly that I could hear it beating and I was drenched in sweat.

I took out my phone and called Tanu. The call was dropped. I called over and over— no reply. The clock's ticking hands and my courage, which were giving me the impression that I was very strong, were powerless to stop the tears from welling up in my eyes. I gave up. I stood up and started crying. My parents approached me.

'I couldn't sleep. What should I do?' I said to my mother. I could not, of course, tell them about Tanu. It wouldn't make sense since she was gone. My father lay down next to me. I thought back to my early years and how I used to sleep next to them in such a manner. Regardless of how mature I appeared to them, they were the ones who knew me the best. I finally got the sleep I had been craving for the past few days when my father fell asleep next to me. Every day, life was offering me something and hitting me in the face.

The next day brought hope for me. Chacha ji finally found a match for me, and the good thing was that I knew this girl, Rashmi. I desperately wanted to talk to someone. We chatted a few years ago. She was preparing for her NET exam. I saw the details and remembered her contact number. I saved her contact number. When the night came, I messaged her. I thought nothing before texting her. I just did.

'Remember me?' I texted. I wanted her to be curious from my first text.

A few minutes later, she replied, 'Oh, Mr. Writer, how are you?'

'Won't you ask from where I got your number?'

'I know. My parents have distributed my resume for a suitable boy.'

'So, you didn't get a text from any other person?'

'I didn't reply to them.'

'How come a smart girl like you didn't find a suitable match?'

'Maybe that was the reason if you think so.'

'That could be true.'

'How come a writer is finding a suitable match through arrange marriages? You always favoured love.'

'Time changes, people change.'

'You didn't get the right ones for you, I suppose.'

'I think the same for you.'

'I was about to get married to a person, then I pulled things back.'

'So, you had a relationship? You could've hidden this part.'

'You could hide it by yourself if it bothers you. Why didn't you get married? Still living in your fantasy world?'

'What's wrong with my fantasy world?'

'Nothing's wrong if it gives you a living. Otherwise, everything's wrong.'

'For livelihood, I have other skills. I teach computer languages and I am learning some advance courses.'

'And.'

'And.... I recently had a breakup...from a nineteen-year-old girl.'

'Nineteen-year-old! Well, you always had that charm of words.'

'Maybe she thought that 'age gap' and 'generation gap' are synonyms for one another,' she said further, followed by a smiley emoji.

'Valid point,' I chuckled.

'Why did you pull off your marriage? It seemed you had a pretty serious relationship with the guy.' I asked.

'He was a chameleon, didn't show his true colours until we got engaged. He asked me to send nude pictures of my cousin while she was taking a bath. As his right on her as his Saali as Aadhi Gharwali.'

'What!! It seems the guy has a desire to taste all the flavors,' I replied with a smiley.

'Then he instructed my mother to get him a bed in the dowry that doesn't make a sound while having sex. He sent me the photo of the bed on which he wanted to have a hardcore sex with me on our wedding night.'

'Some people grow up being assholes. You should inquire about which bed was given to his daughters and sisters.'

'And instead of feeling apologetic for these petty acts. He laughed.'

'I understand. You should thank yourself for saving yourself.'

Our chats began that way, as adult people do, with nothing to hide and everything out in the open, allowing us to discuss anything. Things progressed well, and I could sleep for once. A week later, I decided to give her a call.

Chapter-20

The Time's Demand

For a brief while, we spoke. My eyes were filled with tears. I didn't sense the loss of Tanu when we were texting, but as soon as we spoke, I realized she was another girl. Rashmi was a mature girl. Tanu used to explain her responses to me, but she had all the answers to questions in her own unique style. I was crying silently while listening to her.

'She isn't her. Try once more to bring her back.' I heard my numb heart's voice.

'Listen Rashu, my father is calling. I will talk to you later,' I said and cut the call.

'At least we can talk for once.' I texted Tanu. My heartbeat became erratic after I texted. I tried to unsend the SMS message, but I could not do so. My face was covered in terror. I was waiting impatiently for her response, but I was also terrified of it. One wretched and repulsive response would take me straight back to hell.

'Just go and get married, you old bastard. I have found someone of my age, someone less mature. Grow some balls, don't beg here,' she texted back and sent me directly to hell.

I returned to the hell where I was trying my best to get away from– the hell of frustration, misery, and depression. Corona had eaten up my body and that nineteen-year-old girl who might have died without me, ate up my soul. I was on the verge of my extinction. There was a strong feeling of revenge in my mind. I desperately wanted to text her something penetrative and full of abuse. Then I halted.

'I will definitely get married now. Thanks for the green flag,' I texted back.

I called Rashu again and tried to make a conversation. I knew her voice would be familiar after a few days. We had our grown-up talks and the past talks. Day by day, our talks grew bolder and darker. Within a month, we had discussed everything about love, life, and the future.

After a month, I wished to meet her. She was coming to Rishikesh to visit her aunt, and I was feeling weird because everything was happening so fast. I had deep memories of Rishikesh with Tanu. My heart was in pieces. I wasn't feeling a thing, nothing at all. It was the demand of the time. It was possible that Rashmi couldn't give me the goosebumps and the vibe that I used to get from Tanu, but I was pretty sure that she would definitely give me a good time. She was sorted.

On the agreed-upon day, I set off for Rishikesh. As she suggested, I was waiting for her on the beach near Laxman Jhoola. I was sitting on the same rock. My eyes were hovering here and there hoping a miracle could happen and I could see Tanu. I remembered the Chilla Road and the momos stall where I made fun of her looks, similar to the seller of momos. My heart was collapsing. Suddenly, I felt feverish. Even the beach couldn't provide me with the cold vibes. I was still into her. I was seeing her in the flashes. Every red scooty was reminding me of her.

'What if I didn't forget Tanu even after marriage? It would be an emotional fraud to Rashmi. I should go from here. I can't corrupt her life.' I thought.

'But Tanu has moved on, so I have to move on, too. Now is not the time to be emotional. It is time to move forward strongly, and a promising girl like Rashmi may not be found in the future. Apart from me, she didn't even talk to anyone. She told me everything so clearly. I have to make myself worth it.' I thought again.

My headache began. The purpose of our meeting was supposed to be romantic, but I felt like I would waste it. Then she arrived, clad in a green suit with embroidery around the neck. A female with greater maturity than Tanu. In her hand was a carry bag. She removed her mask. She was literally stunning. I could never really compare her to Tanu. She took a seat next to me, on another rock. We exchanged gentle smiles and didn't speak for a while. The mountain I was focussing on, she was looking there too.

'Did you find anything?' She asked.

'I was hoping you would come from there,' I said.

'And a large vulture would snatch me and carry me here, gliding over this wide river.'

She said in a sarcasm.

We both burst out laughing.

'Why carry a bag?' I asked her.

'Mausi made sandwiches for you,' she said.

'I really am starving.' I took the bag from her and began to devour the sandwiches.

'Oh sorry, you look so pretty. I was about to say that first,' I said.

She laughed.

'Hunger comes first before anything,' she said.

'I had a memory of this place.'

'Now, it's replaced,' she said. 'Time for creating fresh memories.'

We roamed around the places and spent a lovely time together. While I was with her, she drove me into a more romantic realm. She introduced me to more popular food items there. She was a core lover of Rishikesh. I presumed to be a tough boy in front of her. I didn't show that I'm still a fragile person who was afraid of being alone. We were standing at a momos stall in Shiv Puri.

'He is still texting me to forgive him,' she said, mentioning about his ex-fiancé.

'So, didn't you give it a second thought?' I asked.

'Doesn't that bother you if I give him a second chance?' she asked.

'I just want you to clear your clutter. Of course, it would bother me if I lose you, but what would bother me more is that if you think about giving him a second chance later,' I said.

'Even though he had been in my life for the previous three years, I still had to put in a lot of effort to persuade him to see things my way. He had his work, and I was his loyal girlfriend. He never valued my perspective. While you, in the past one month, I didn't think I had to make an effort to make you understand something. You have more neurons active in your brain, while his half brain was shut off,' she said.

'So, you have made your decision,' I said.

'Do you have any doubt?' She asked.

'No, let's take this relationship further,' I said.

'No, no, not so soon. You are not ready.' A voice came from inside.

As we hiked across the slopes and uphill, we followed a narrow path. Holding her hands in mine, I felt a sense of comfort. Given the path's damaged condition, I assumed we would be alone. Standing beneath a distant tree, far from the road, I gently leaned in towards her lips. Surprisingly, she did not hesitate, and I planted a kiss on her glossy red lips. My intention was for this kiss to erase any memory of Tanu, as I longed to move forward and have Rashmi's lips imprint upon mine. I couldn't resist giving her another kiss, but it didn't feel quite right. Perhaps she didn't feel entirely comfortable in that moment.

'We should go back now,' she said.

Our paths diverged when we reached the bus stop. I hopped on a bus while she headed to her own. I got home very late at night. Thanks to the meeting, I could unwind and relax. I now have someone to talk to about things to strike up a discussion.

Gradually, my days underwent a transformation. Life now felt stable. Throughout the day, I would diligently work on my lectures, tend to household chores, and engage in late-night conversations with Rashmi over the phone. Even during moments of silence, we would keep the call connected, creating a sense of togetherness. Whenever she brewed tea, I would envision her actions as she placed the earphones in her ears. It always brought a smile to my face when she playfully crushed ginger. Our calls would span from nine in the evening until around midnight. On several occasions, when my mother called, Rashmi would mimic her voice, adding a touch of humour to our conversations. Gradually, everything began to fall into place. Within a mere two months, we had grown incredibly close, and she openly embraced my provocative talks, always responding with a smile.

'So, you had this too, in you. I thought you were a pure romantic, less dirty,' she used to say.

'We should meet properly if you want to see how dirty I am,' I said.

She giggled.

'Someone is getting an erection,' she said once.

'Why don't you calm this excited erected guy?' I replied.

I just want to override every memory of Tanu. While I fantasize about kissing Rashmi or getting intimate with her in my dreams, Tanu interrupted me. That's why I needed to replace her. So, I requested Rashmi if we could spend some private moment.

'Someone is in such a hurry,' she teased me.

'I just want to smell you, want to roll my fingers on your belly button, want to write my names on your spine with my tongue for you to identify.'

'And...' she said, wondrously.

'I want to love you in infinite ways, starting from the tiny wrinkles on your forehead.'

'And...'

'Going down and down...and we could enter the world of lusty pleasure as an outcome of our pure love and serenity.'

'A writer has his own way of saying that he wants to make love to someone,' she said.

I burst out laughing.

'We should wait. I don't want things to go fast,' she said.

'Patience is a quality I possess. I just want to feel the orgasm of Everest,' I said.

'We should wait...' she said.

'It's okay.'

That night, I received a message.

'That rolling finger on the belly button you were saying, I could feel it on my belly button and felt like tickling,' she said.

'It's awesome, and it will make you wild.' I enhanced her excitement.

'Come next week, let me feel the wild,' she said.

We had a lot of nasty chats.

'A person who never had sex can live without it, whether he is in his twenties or thirties or any stage of his life. However, once someone has experienced it, it becomes extremely difficult for them to resist,' she said.

'Absolutely, it becomes a part of living,' I said.

'In the present-day, many people are actively engaging in hookup culture. The common practice, as they say, is to count the number of bodies and then share it with friends. They call it body count.'

'Are you enquiring me about my body count?'

'No, I don't mean it in that way.'

'Teenagers and young adults, they do what the trend asks them to do. Their goal is to feel exceptional each day.

They have a strong desire to have sex as frequently as they can. Right now, they have no desire for stability in their life.'

We exchanged our knowledge on every topic we had in our mind. She was a perfect match for me. We even had a long discussion over dowry and how the marriage of children has always been a costly venture for a middle-class father. He set aside cash for this, cuts off the majority of his desires. The costs of marriage could shake his financial stability. Particularly, if he is planning his daughter's wedding. He is anxious and attempts to win over the guests at the groom's side. He wants his daughter to have a secure future. Though I don't know many fathers, a father's greatest love is for his daughter.

The thing what was inside my mind was that Rashmi never forced or aspired me to be someone that I wasn't. She was smart. I was certain that, should she decide to marry me, she would pick me for who I am, not for the professional title I hold, unlike nowadays where people are marrying for the jobs or designation of the person, not the person.

Following our decision to meet up, I immediately went to see her in person and took care of all the necessary hotel arrangements.

Initially, we reclined in bed and engaged in some absurd small talk. She could sense that I wasn't initiating the romance, since I was a little bashful about where to begin. The cabinet had a long mirror next to it. I had a thought.

'Let's see, how do we look together in front of the mirror?'

Her eyes sparkled. We got up and stood there.

'You're 5'3,' I said.

'And you are 5'9.'

'If I stand behind you, I can see my face,' I said and stood behind her.

While standing in front of the mirror, we shared a moment of connection as our eyes met. Gently, I reached out and rested my hand on her waist, causing her to softly close her eyes. I approached her from behind gently, wrapping my arms around her in a warm embrace, and placing tender kisses on her neck. The sensation of her warm breaths against my nose was both surprising and comforting. I gently guided her towards me, turning her body to face mine, and then I leaned in to kiss her tenderly. Initiating with a gentle kiss, I maintained the act of kissing her without interruption. Her eyes widened, giving me the impression that she wanted me to push forward. I carefully lifted her off the ground and gently placed her on the soft bed. I engaged in a continuous act of kissing and licking her lips and neck.

'Let's do it,' I said.

'I want to tell you something,' she said.

'Don't tell me you're a boy down there.'

Both of us laughed.

'This is not my first time,' she said.

'Neither is mine and it is our first time. Let's remember it like that.'

She gently smiled.

'Let's do it then.'

We undressed each other. She saw my hairy chest.

'Someone inherited more testosterone from his ancestors,' she said, and nuzzled her hand over my chest.

'A bear,' she said.

'My ex used to call me grizzly. She used to add 'my' too,' I said.

'Still miss her?' She stared at me.

I didn't reply.

'Not after today.' After uttering those words, she wasted no time grabbing hold of my vest, forcefully tugging me along with her. As per our phone conversation, I followed through with all the actions we discussed. I was completely captivated by her stunning physique, cherishing every inch of her remarkable body. The allure of every curve on her body was overwhelming, compelling me to love her endlessly. Not only was she incredibly cooperative, but she also knew exactly how to make it the best it could be. Without exaggeration, I can confidently say that it was the most incredible sexual experience I have ever had. The exertion of our physical activity caused both of us to break into sweat, and following that, she sought comfort in my arms.

'I want this for the rest of my life,' I said.

'Me too,' she said, with a sweet gesture on her face.

'Let's get engaged. Rashu, I have a desire to marry you.'

'I want to marry you too, Jay.'

'Tonight, I plan on informing my parents about this so that they don't arrange a marriage for me with someone else.'

'Same here.'

'Let's get married.'

We had come to a mutual understanding and accepted each other. Allowing her into my life, I eagerly embraced the love she poured onto me, filling the emptiness that had once consumed me. With our stomachs growling, we eagerly made our way to Domino's, craving the taste of their delicious pizza. With our stomachs full from devouring the onion cheese pizza, we exchanged heartfelt goodbyes and went our separate ways. Memories of her filled my thoughts as I sat on the bus, lost in reverie.

I arrived home and stood behind my father, who was watering the plants.

'I want to marry Rashmi,' I said.

'You met her today?' He asked.

My parents knew I was talking to a girl since last month.

'Yes, I met her properly, and we had a lot of discussions. She is a perfect match for me,' I explained.

'But we were going to finalize another girl. Just have a look,' he said with a bit of worry over his forehead.

'No, no, I am going to marry this girl and we should start preparations. Meet her parents and talk to them,' I said.

'So, our opinion doesn't concern you,' he said in a fatherly voice.

'I have made my decision. I have chosen the girl on the list you provided,' I said.

Since we haven't received a response from you, we have already decided,' said father.

'And don't tell me you have arranged the meeting too,' I spoke in an unusually loud voice.

'Not yet.'

'Good, I'm going to marry this girl,' I said.

My brother was happier than me. It didn't take long for everyone to find out that I had made my decision and chosen the girl. I picked up the phone and dialled Rashmi's number, informing her that my father was looking to have a conversation with her. With her eloquent speech, she successfully charmed my father and effectively persuaded him we were an ideal match for one another.

Subsequently, my father engaged in a discussion with Rashmi's parents. Nothing went wrong and everything was in order.

Chapter-21

A New Beginning?

Amidst the grip of the corona fever, I shed 8 to 10 kilos of weight. My once plump face had transformed. My chest and belly aligned harmoniously, as if they whispered secrets to each other in the night's quiet when I was ill. Yet, my arms had weakened too. Within a mere month, our hearts entwined, and we exchanged promises and got engaged. In Rashmi's family, I found acceptance. Their eyes held no judgment, only love. The days between our engagement and the wedding were like stolen moments—precious and fleeting. Each encounter deepened our connection, weaving threads of trust and shared dreams. Tanu, once vivid and all-consuming, now lingered like a faded photograph in the dusty corners of my mind and heart. Rashmi's love was a new realm. It was a love reaching depths I hadn't known existed. Tanu, once the sun, had become a distant star, its light dimmed by the brilliance of a new dawn.

I had sent an invitation to Tanu's mother over WhatsApp. She did not respond. Three months later, on my wedding day, my friends and loved ones enjoyed themselves to the fullest. All of my relatives were present, blessing me as I sat in the chariot — a vessel of destiny.

Most of them were drunk and dancing furiously in front of my chariot. As is customary at Indian weddings, the road had become their dance floor. After completing all the Hindu ceremonies, I married Rashmi. The air hummed with anticipation, and as the vermilion marked my forehead, a new world unfurled—a world of shared responsibilities and intertwined fates. In the days that followed, I realized that this union was more than vows and rituals. It was a pact with existence itself—a promise to navigate life's currents together. With Rashmi by my side, I stepped into the uncharted territory of matrimony, ready to shoulder the weight of our shared dreams and build a life that would endure beyond the fleeting dance of celebration.

I stepped into a new job; my days were no longer confined to make lectures. Life quickened its pace, and I found myself juggling responsibilities. While I dedicated myself in keeping our home afloat, she immersed herself in exam preparations. Our nights were a symphony of shared moments—movies and freshly minted web series, laughter, and whispered secrets. And then there were those nights—the ones that persisted like the aftertaste of a sweet dessert. After the warmth of our lovemaking, we'd dive into conversations that knew no bounds. The clock would tiptoe toward 4 a.m., and our words would create an array of dreams and speculations. Those late-night conversations became our routine, a private world we shared beneath the moonlight.

Rashmi, with her captivating presence, cast a spell that rekindled my love for a simple rural life. My old friends summoned me to play cricket in a sun-drenched field like I used to play. There, I gained fame for my unpredictable batting—sometimes hitting triumphant fours or soaring sixes, and other times facing embarrassing outs. I disliked the mundane running for a single or double. My village had little stalls for Chinese food and I used to bring it for her. And then there was her—cherished like warm parcels of noodles and dumplings. In her gaze, I transformed from a mere person into a devoted partner.

Those nine months blurred into a canvas of shared laughter, whispered secrets, and stolen glances. My world shrank to the confines of our love, and I embraced it. My parents, with warm hearts, approved. Their once carefree wanderer son had found his anchor. As the sun dipped below the distant forest, I knew I was home, not just in the village, but within the sanctuary of Rashmi's heart.

For someone like me, it is difficult to sustain or acclimate to the typical speed of life. I consider the past nine months of my life to be a honeymoon period, where everything felt blissful and perfect. Following that, a former acquaintance of mine offered me a job opportunity. Haridwar was the designated location for this job. The pay scale for this offer was incredibly impressive, so accepting it would undoubtedly ensure that we have a prosperous and comfortable life. A shockwave rushed through me when I came across the word 'Haridwar' while reading. Rashmi was absolutely thrilled when she read the offer letter. I was offered the opportunity to be assigned as an Assistant Professor at the university, and to further support my academic journey, they also offered me a fellowship to pursue my doctorate degree.

'We will definitely go there,' she insisted.

'Let me share this news with our parents,' I said.

I discussed this with my parents, and I was partially pleased with the offer, but I was concerned about why I wasn't completely satisfied.

'Haridwar still haunts me,' I thought.

I went to the washroom and ended up spending the next forty-five minutes there. At this moment, I found myself sitting on the toilet seat, eyes closed. Upon coming out, I found myself once again in Tanu's world. The scratches on her scooty were so visible that they appeared to be hovering right before my eyes. The thought of my first kiss with her brought back a rush of nostalgia and emotions. The memories of how things used to be before I contracted corona were still fresh in my mind. All the memories from my past that I had left behind suddenly resurfaced and played vividly in front of my eyes. I had the impression that I had concealed it in the cupboard and then something unexpectedly opened it. This offer letter had brought about a profound change in me, and I was not the person I was prior to its arrival. Feeling lost, I was comforted when Rashmi brought me a cup of tea. 'Here is your tea. Special ginger-flavoured.' She spoke.

I looked at her face. I felt less close to her that day. I was not feeling loyal. My emotions had simply changed towards my past. She softly slapped me.

'Where are you? Confused about the job?' She asked.

'No, nothing,' I said.

'Crazy man,' she said and left.

'Should I take this job? What if something bad happened to me there? What if Tanu meets Rashmi someday?' I thought.

I was desperately missing her red scooty. That scooty was pulling me harder than Tanu herself.

Something went wrong for me that night while we were making love. Rashmi's face reminded me of Tanu, and I almost had a stroke. I placed my hand over my chest and turned to the opposite side. Rashmi grew panicked.

'What happened?'

'Nothing, just a muscle strain,' I said and then I ran to the bathroom. I was gasping again. I punched the tiles of the bathroom and cried in the corner.

'What's happening to me? Why didn't you go away?' I spoke.

Before it was too late, I wiped my tears and went back to her. That was the first time we were laying in the bed silently, halfway through.

Over the next two days, I experienced a significant hindrance in conversing with Rashmi, as my attention was constantly diverted, leaving my soul unsettled. My mind was consumed with thoughts of Tanu, wondering where she might be and what she might have achieved by now. Because of this behaviour, Rashmi became upset and refused to speak to me as well. She was simply performing the formalities with no genuine interest or enthusiasm. On the third day, I approached Rashmi.

'Pack the bags. We will shift to Haridwar,' I said.

'So, you were confused about the job for the past few days?'

'I needed to figure out pros and cons of the job.'

I informed my mother and father of this decision. My brother was overjoyed since we were going to live together, and now he did not have to worry about his meals.

We moved to Haridwar. The joining was two days later, so I visited all the major places with Rashmi, where Tanu and I used to go. I tried to override Tanu's memory with Rashmi. That evening, we were eating dosa at the same location, and the stall owner recognized me. He asked me, 'Where is the other girl?' I grinned back but didn't provide an answer. A week later, the same thing happened at the biryani shop. He asked me the same thing. Because Tanu and I had shared countless memorable experiences, I found it challenging to create new ones. I asked the biryani shop owner about her.

'She comes occasionally with a boy. She might not live here,' he said.

'Did you ever ask her about me?'

'Yes, she said you got married.'

The city of Haridwar, which is Tanu's hometown, had warmly welcomed both me and my wife. Our weekends were always filled with visits to temples and exploring the most enchanting places. The time we spent in Chilla, Rishikesh was incredibly enjoyable and we had a lot of fun. I did everything possible to forget her. We had the incredible opportunity to spend three months in this stunning and spiritually significant city. Over the course of the last few days, my mother joined us and stayed with us.

'Now you need to shift home. She can't stay here in such conditions,' she said.

'What condition?' I glanced at Rashmi's face with a curiosity.

'She is pregnant.' Mother said, observed my face.

At first, I wasn't sure how to react to this news. We had not planned for this, so everything came as a surprise. When I looked at her face, she appeared to be surprised too. I wasn't ready to be a father, but God had plans for us that only He knew about. I accepted my fate and urged myself to prepare for this surprise. Mother ordered me to either move home or send her home, and I didn't want to leave Haridwar until I found inner peace and answers to my unsolved life mysteries. However, time had demanded me to prioritize something more significant than these trivial matters of the heart.

'We will distribute our work. I can't let her go. How would I manage? She will definitely need me too,' I said.

'Then you have to be very careful in the first trimester,' Mother said.

Learning about her pregnancy intensified my concerns for both my wife and my career. Intending to provide them with the best life, I developed new plans. Initially, I chose a doctor for her and subsequently reached out to my cousin in order to help her. I would wake up early to lend a hand with various chores for her, and once I returned from work, we would engage in a plethora of enjoyable activities, engaging in conversations, and watching delightful movie nights. Life had nearly regained its usual rhythm and pace. There was a momentary pause in the activities happening inside. Over time, a pattern had been steadily developing. Once again, I found myself deeply committed and dedicated to the routine, causing everything else to fade into the background for a period. As time went on, my love for her continued to grow even more, especially knowing that she was carrying a precious life within her.

We have cherished every moment of the nine-month journey of her pregnancy, considering it a truly golden time. It was a regular occurrence for me to examine her swollen belly at the start of each month. The name of our baby is something we discussed during our late-night conversations. It was quite interesting for me to observe the entire process of a woman's pregnancy, from the physical changes in her body to the fluctuating moods she experiences. I witnessed every single thing that happened with Rashmi. Prior to her delivery, I took a break from my job. There wasn't a specific motive behind my resignation.

I simply stepped down. The long-awaited moment finally arrived, and we were filled with joy when we were blessed with the birth of a precious baby girl. The doctor reached out to me and gently placed in my arms a precious child who was having a difficult time adapting to life in this world. With great effort, she was vigorously tossing her legs and struggling to pry open her eyes. It was at that precise moment, when she cried in my arms, that I realized I never wanted it to end. We named her Avni. My eyes welled up with tears, and that everyone, even my father, saw her was almost surreal. I never imagined that we could make our parents so happy. Both of them were playing with their granddaughter. My phone flooded with messages and calls. Those who could come did and wished us well.

Once again, I decided to shift back to my village and reconnect with my former friend by rejoining our former work. Our home had undergone a remarkable transformation, now brimming with her adorable little clothes, toys, diapers, wipes, and an array of other baby-related belongings that were entirely new to us. Yet, rather than feeling overwhelmed, we were filled with a sense of wonder and enthusiasm at the prospect of this new chapter in our lives. During that time, it became our habit to wait for her whenever she laughed. My parents had entered the new realm of being grandparents. It took me four months to fully understand the swiftness with which time was passing. The continuous nature of it means that it never stops, which in turn brings about changes not only within yourself but also among the surrounding people.

Chapter-22

The Deadlock

On that particular day, I was lying in bed, casually using my phone while my daughter, Avni, peacefully slept next to me. I received a message on Instagram. At first, I believed it was a joke, but I later discovered that the message came from Neetu, Tanu's former friend. Her question revolved around her current whereabouts. Obviously, I didn't know either. Neetu asked me to pass on a message to Tanu, expressing how much she missed her and wanted to talk urgently. I couldn't say no because I didn't want Neetu to find out any information about me or Tanu. The entire conversation flooded my mind even after she exited the chat.

The next thought that occurred to me left me perplexed.

'Again, texting her might lead me to hell. What if Neetu did something wrong to her, which was significant enough to end their friendship? After all, I know she wasn't on good terms with her buddies.' I thought.

'What if Neetu is my chance to make peace with her? I can reach her on behalf of Neetu.' I thought again.

'It was your friend, Neetu. She wants to talk to you urgently. I believe she is your old friend and you should listen to what she has to say.' I texted.

Now was the time to wait for her response. I wasn't afraid she'd hit my heart, but I was anxious. My desire was for her to respond casually. I wanted her to understand that life is too short to dwell on hatred. We should make peace instantly. I just put my phone away and lay down next to my Avni. I was about to shut my eyes.

A couple of minutes later, I received a text. I was sleepy.

'Did she say anything in particular?'

When I glanced at her message, it didn't appear to be genuine or authentic. My inner state was filled with such disorientation that my mind couldn't comprehend the fact that she messaged me in the exact casual manner I had longed for just a couple of minutes earlier. It turned out that what I thought was happening was just a daydream. For the second time, I placed the phone out of sight. I expected her to respond with hatred and possibly abuse.

'You should check your phone once more,' my inner voice fell upon my ears.

'There is nothing to check. Just sleep,' my lethargic mind said.

'What if she's for real?'

I was half-asleep and my mind was racing. My eyelids did not want to rise.

'It would be a random number which ends in 63, not hers.'

'But it ends in 63.'

My eyes instantly went wide in amazement. I spun back to look at the text, which was from her. What an excitement! Shame on me!

'Not in particular. Just wanted to talk to you,' I texted.

'Don't want snakes in my life. Finally, my life is sorted,' she replied.

'Make sure you don't regret mistaking someone for a snake. Sometimes we decide based on our assumptions, but the truth is significantly more different,' I said.

'I'm okay with my decisions.'

'Still the stubborn child.'

'I'm not a child anymore. People like you and her made me an adult before my time.'

'Then you should be thankful to both of us.'

She didn't reply after this. I read all the messages again. What I concluded was that she wanted an actual conversation that would be suitable for her.

'Should I message again?' I asked to myself.

I didn't. She touched the nerve again.

'She could have chosen not to respond, but she did. Maybe she has something to say.'

I kept reviewing her texts nonstop. I was trying to determine if she wanted to make me feel bad or if she was just introducing the subject. I was analysing her messages too much.

'What if she wants me to suffer more?'

'What if she had something to say that she wasn't able to say that time?'

'What if she wanted to be a normal person to me? Like nothing happened.'

'What if she misses me for the wonderful memory we created?'

'What if she is still in trouble and wants some advice?'

My brain was just going crazy. Once again, I found myself stuck in a loophole.

I typed a message.

'I am curious about what my brother told you that day regarding my marriage and myself.'

She didn't reply.

I consoled myself by assuming she was busy or doing something, but I knew she had read this message, and I received three consecutive texts that night.

'You ended up proving him right with whatever he said about you. Now that we have gone our separate ways, I feel a sense of calm.'

'We should be like we were before. That version of you was way better than...you know.'

'If that madness hadn't happened between us, we would have surely attended your wedding and had a great time.'

'It's working.' I thought.

'So, you regret falling in love with me?' I asked.

'I don't want to discuss this. When I remember all of this, I just hate you. You seemed to take advantage of us, particularly me. After you, I decided I would not keep any toxic people in my life,' she replied.

'You know the reason.' I texted.

'Have you become what you wanted to? Even you deceived yourself too,' she said.

And that line hit me hard.

'At least you had a spark back then,' she texted further.

I threw my phone. It hit the wall and its screen broke.

Avni and Rashmi both woke up. Avni started crying.

'What's wrong with you? I've been watching you since last night. Either you quit doing this or walk to another room to figure out what's bothering you. Just let us sleep,' Rashmi screamed.

Glancing at her face, I noticed and took up my phone. I moved to another room. I was burning from within. She had again sent me into hell. I looked at the screen. It still functioned. The cover had shattered. I removed the cover and began typing.

'You're blaming me for whatever I've done. Have you considered it for your own sake? Picture how your life would have been without me during your most crucial times. I witnessed your mother's emotional breakdown when there was no romantic involvement between us. Despite your family turning their back on you, I stood by your side, expecting nothing in return. I was not a thief, a fraudster, or someone with malicious intentions. The time was not right. That's why I did it, hoping that I could correct it later.'

'Your hatred was stronger than your love. I became extremely frail following my battle with COVID-19. None of you showed any empathy towards the fact that that task could have been completed within a few days. Despite my inability to come, you still compelled me. You didn't give me a fair chance to be heard, treating me as if I were a proper criminal. Threatened to file a police complaint. Had I been under your control, you would have tortured and killed me.'

'After listening to my brother, you simply walked away without saying a word. Even before I agreed to marry, you had already moved on to another relationship. My intention was always to not speak or justify myself, as I held onto the belief that one day you would grasp the truth. However, you persisted in cursing me. Saying that I used all of you.'

I put my phone away after saying this. My peace had vanished. My priorities shifted again. I got involved in her knowing that this turbulence inside my heart would keep dragging me deeper into this miserable hell. Despite my desire to walk away from all of this garbage, I found myself stuck once more. I was unaware of the devil's plan for me. It appeared that God had abandoned me.

She didn't text me afterwards, nor did I. I just conveyed the message that I so desired. I wanted to elaborate to her twenty-year-old mind that I was not the villain that she had accused me of. I just wanted serenity and focus on my family and career. For the next few days, I acted like a normal person and avoided being a freak in my bedroom.

'Have I truly deceived myself? Is she correct?'

'What about the stories' drafts that were rusting in the folders?'

Next day, after preparing the lecture, I opened the folder that hadn't been opened in two years. Most people on this planet had given up on their dreams because they had to settle to sustain a necessary life. To earn for their family and to provide. Like Gus says in Breaking Bad, *'A man always provides whether or not he was praised or awarded for this.'* Pursuing dreams can be less challenging for someone who is alone. If the dream is ambitious, a person might push himself to the limit and beyond, despite the hardships. However, when there are people depending upon you, it becomes nearly impossible.

I aspired to be a writer and novelist, and that was the thing Tanu knew more deeply than Rashmi. Rashmi mistook it for my hobby since I never demonstrated a clear commitment to this goal of mine. So, I had to make adjustments to my plans. This time I planned to quit the education industry permanently and join the publishing industry. As I opened the folder, I saw my incomplete stories and blogs.

I looked for institutions and firms that specialize in content development, blog writing, and article writing. I applied for many positions. On a daily basis, I would apply for 5-6 positions that were relevant to me. I reopened one of my incomplete projects and resumed to work on it. A 30-year-old unemployed man in northern India is deemed wicked by middle-class households. I had been a computer science lecturer at two institutions, and I'd had enough of the sheep mentality.

Before the birth of my beautiful daughter, I left the job so that I could find my peace in my village, where I could live beside my family. I wanted to work nearby my village so that I could take care of my family, but when Tanu reminded me whether or not I was pursuing my ambition and it felt extremely agonizing. I've always had discussions about my aspirations to open my own publication house and become a successful author. My desire was to sit beside rivers and mountains.

A week later, I received a call from Prestige Publication inviting me to an interview in Dehradun. I told Rashmi about my plans to fulfil my ambition. She was a little unhappy because I was earning a decent wage at my former institution, and we all know that chasing dreams is regarded as a gloomy affair in our middle-class world. She realized my crazy side even before we married, so she didn't dispute with her little lunatic spouse.

'How would you earn? They won't pay you well just for writing,' she said, worrying about me.

'They won't pay me well now, but they will. I will show them something extraordinary,' I replied. And that's how I convinced my wife.

The following day, I came to Dehradun and stood in front of the Police Line Headquarters in front of Prestige Publishing House to discuss my next novel and to get freelancing or part-time employment. I recalled a time when I was completely free and made over 90% of my own decisions. Following my interview, I had a strong desire to eat the delicious chicken korma and stew from Delhi Darbar. The day was gorgeous. Moving at its own pace, the city continued. The roads were congested, and the crossroads and intersections had been recently renovated. The city appeared to be more attractive.

At 1 pm, the restaurant was quiet and unhurried. The pleasing smell of the korma was just hitting my nostrils, and my mouth was filled with saliva. As I already stated, the day was intuitive; my senses were expecting something to happen, and I witnessed something I should not have and quickly halted. Two seats away from me, there was a girl whose hair caught my eye as she faced straight, while the boy she was seated with chuckled and waited for their orders. He tapped the table repeatedly while the car's key dangled from his thumb. The girl's hair looked familiar, but I needed to confirm her identity based on the order she offered them.

Along with the roasted chicken leg pieces, there was a big Pepsi, a plate of biryani, and extra leg piece and chilly chicken. I didn't glimpse her, but it was definitely Tanu.

'Is it God's plan? Or a coincidence? Or a miracle?'

Since it was lunchtime on Wednesday, it's possible that she had a craving for chicken. However, what made this incident coincidental was that she happened to be in the same restaurant. A thought suddenly popped into my mind. I mentioned that restaurant to her before. Therefore, I realized that I had accidentally given her the address for Wednesday's lunch. It wasn't a mere coincidence. The result was a direct outcome of my influential tongue. It was obvious that she lived close to this restaurant and visited here every Wednesday.

The only thing she ate was the leg piece, nothing more. I felt a momentary pang in my heart. The boy and she were both in their early twenties, and he was staring at me just as I was staring at them. He mentioned something about me to her. Before she could turn back, I concealed my face by resting another arm on the table. A couple of seconds later I saw them with thieved eye and he wasn't looking at me anymore. I wasn't staring at them. I just wanted to observe one more thing —if she would pour Pepsi into the glass or not. As our eyes connected, he swiftly came to me.

'Is there an issue you have with us?' He inquired. Clearly, he was an obsessive lover and he couldn't digest someone staring at his girlfriend. He stood before me, obstructing my sight. I moved a bit and noticed a glass full of Pepsi. I softly chuckled.

'Sorry, what were you saying?' I asked him. As I continued to ignore him, he grew increasingly humiliated and angry.

'Why are you smiling?' He made intense eye contact, like in movie fight scenes.

'I've seen no one order so many chicken leg pieces. I was pondering how you would eat them all,' I said.

He got paused for a second. Then he laughed.

'She is the mischievous little devil over there. Is there really nothing else besides this mysterious leg piece theory?' He asked.

When I pressed my mobile unlock button, my daughter's and wife's wallpapers lit up.

'My entire world revolves around them. Nothing else matters to me. I hope you can comprehend this,' I said.

He cleared the clutter, returned to his seat, and I hastened to a hidden corner to avoid gossip. Still, my heart wasn't accepting that she was there. It went numb.

Before she could spot me, I hurriedly came outside after finishing my lunch. Therefore, I lit a cigarette and observed a new EV bus go by. "Go Green" and "Zero Emission" were largely imprinted on it. I received a call from the publication house. I delicately held a half-burnt cigarette as we talked about the position they wished for me to propose. While I requested gum from the shopkeeper, I noticed Tanu was standing next to me, asking for a water bottle. Her eyes locked onto mine. The cigarette dropped. Her boyfriend was standing hardly five steps from her.

We didn't talk or make eye contact afterward. I started my bike and swiftly left. I was driving aimlessly when I decided to take a detour to Kimadi village in search of a quiet location in the mountains to rest and relax. And again, like zombies rising from the grave, feelings that I believed were long gone returned. The heart that was numb a few moments ago found itself blossoming.

'How come this is happening?' I thought.

'This felt like cheating on my wife, I shouldn't feel like this.' I thought.

'Maybe temporary, like we fall for some random person for a few minutes.'

I constantly felt like my head was experiencing a CPU deadlock in terms of computer science.

I received a text on my Instagram.

'Fatherhood looks good on you.'

I knew who the text was from. I simply read and dismissed it from my notification. The way that coincidence happened left me completely astonished. And why?

I returned to my home. The entire journey was brightened by the memory I shared with her again.

Rashmi was lying in bed right next to me. She fell asleep a few minutes later, and I was about to do the same. Right before I drift off and close my eyes, a notification's sound ruined everything. I received a message on Instagram, and I picked up the phone.

'Was it just a coincidence or were you really looking for me?'

I knew who the message came from. Even though I acknowledged the message multiple times, I still felt uncertain about my emotions. I examined my heart rate. I woke up and washed my face to make sure I didn't sound too eager when replying to her message.

I discovered I wasn't excited, just slightly curious.

'Pure coincidence,' I replied.

'Had I been at your place, I would have said hello to you the moment I laid eyes on you,' she wrote.

'I didn't want to ruin your lunch with your handsome man,' I replied.

'You may be 10 years older, but you taught me the things that transcend age. I would be delighted,' she wrote.

'It seems like something is still weighing on your mind,' she wrote further.

'Unfortunately, our trip to Dehradun didn't happen as planned. We were going to have a trip where we could sit by a waterfall, grill chicken on a gas stove. You promised to have your first drink with me,' I replied.

'By the way, how's your daughter doing?' She abruptly shifted the conversation away from the trip.

'Everything's fine.'

'Okay, bye.'

Right as I was about to say goodbye, she blocked me.

'Shitty person. Still expects me to greet her first.' I thought.

Chapter-23

One Last Journey

During breakfast, with my wife serving and my daughter playing next to me, I had the urge to share the conversation with her, but decided not to. While I was preparing for my approaching interview and revising my resume, she messaged me again.

'I'll accompany you to fulfil my promise one last time. It may not be my first time drinking, but with you, it would seem like the first,' she wrote.

I didn't give a response. My system came to a complete halt. I had conflicting feelings towards her — wanting to strangle her, but also wanting to maintain a normal relationship. I had been looking forward to seeing her and having a conversation a few weeks ago. I was currently experiencing difficulty in deciding what exactly I desired. I didn't feel any pain or animosity towards her boyfriend, either.

'What on earth you want from this world, Jay?'

'You're married and have a daughter. Stop fantasizing about Tanu.'

'Just go and slap her. She wanted to meet you. Avenge your feelings.'

After thirty minutes, she wrote, 'My partner wouldn't be happy to see me chatting with my ex.'

Still, I didn't reply.

'Maldevta will be the place where your fantasies will be realized,' she wrote further.

I unzipped my college bag from years before and found my old pen drive. Since Tanu left, I haven't laid a finger on it. I originally planned for it to rust and never work on any machine. My wife kept a careful eye on me while I held our daughter. Upon opening the drive, I found that everything inside was undisturbed. The last photo captured our journey to Shivpuri, Rishikesh. Furthermore, I came across a note, specifically in the concluding paragraph, where I recalled our most beautiful kiss. I quickly retrieved the disk, and a sense of anxiety overtook my calmness.

'What's on this drive that caused such a traumatic reaction on your face?' I heard Rashmi's voice.

'Some old stuff... nothing important,' I muttered.

'Would you mind if I see your old things? You behave like your past had something...terrible,' she said.

I halted for a moment. 'See it any time you want,' I said.

I placed the pen drive inside my laptop bag.

'Is it possible for you to go without letting your boyfriend know?' I texted Tanu.

'He's a boyfriend, not the husband,' she replied after a few minutes.

Initially, it felt like I was cheating on my wife and I was doing it regardless, keeping the guilt inside my heart. Tanu was the girl with all the good vibes. The places didn't captivate me, but when she was around, they did. After marriage, I had no desire to ever meet her in my entire life. She revealed the true colours of the leaves, which were previously unseen. She caused blossoming flowers and the canvas of Rishikesh's beach sand. In my own mystical way, I loved the turbulence she brought to my path towards heaven. However, the pen drive was meant to be my legacy. It was evident when I fell deeply in love. That pen drive was reminiscent of a time machine for me. As I opened a picture, I was transported back in time. My fear stemmed from my wife's knowledge of this time machine.

One last journey and my legacy with this pen drive will be fulfilled. And I had the intention to do it, regardless.

'Tomorrow 10 am, ISBT,' I texted her.

She viewed the message and responded with a thumbs-up emoji.

The following day, I arrived at the location. The excess crowd made it difficult for me to recognize her, but one thing I recognized immediately was her red scooty.

That scooty filled my mood with joy and happiness. It was parked opposite to the road, and Tanu wasn't there. A bag, which contained all the stuff we needed for the day, was hanging from the hook of the scooty. I crossed the road and nuzzled my hand over its headlight. It had more scratches over it, but for one moment, I thought it was alive.

'So many memories.' I thought.

Tanu watched me rubbing it.

'It's old and rusty,' she complemented.

'Yes, but it has seen so many things, ran on so many terrains. It has had a wonderful life,' I said.

'Drive, we are short on time,' she said.

'To be honest, being with you feels like a betrayal to my wife,' I said.

'You could tell her afterwards or now,' she said.

'As far as I know you, if you call it a cheating, you would still do it. You always do what you have to do regardless of the outcomes,' she added.

'That's me. I don't even know myself.'

'Your daughter laughs like you.'

'Oh…someone's stalking me on Instagram. I heard somewhere that firstborn daughter is the female copy of her father,' I said.

She smiled, as she knew who I was referring to.

We arrived at the stunning Maldevta and settled by the waterfall. My face finally blossomed with a smile that I had been waiting for.

'Despite multiple visits to Dehradun and Mussoorie, it never crossed my mind to come here. It seemed I was destined to come here with you,' I said.

I looked around. The Maldevta Waterfall seemed to be a serene, secluded, and blissful place. It was truly a sight to behold, with its stunning natural surroundings of lush green mountains. The ultimate relaxation in the embrace of nature. The bank of Song River was well known for its recreational activities, making it a popular place to visit. Including a scenic bridge, captivating waterfall, lush farms, feasible camping sites, and historic temples create an added appeal that draws in travellers from far and wide. The mountains in this area, despite their low elevation, make it a highly preferred destination for people who want to experience the beauty of green mountain peaks from such a proximity. The high-pressure water stream falling onto your head offers a meditational and tranquil experience.

Seated on the stones, we took a moment to enjoy the refreshing taste of our beers, and then proceeded to meticulously prepare the spices and gather the required materials for cooking our chicken. Subsequently, we ignited the stove. While our chicken was cooking, we could hear the delightful sound of birds chirping.

'You never told me what my brother told you, exactly?' I asked.

'Why didn't you ask your brother?' She said, her eyelids heavy. The beer seemed to have cast its spell.

'He won't tell,' I said.

'He said that I shouldn't have fallen in love with you. The point was not whether or not you were wrong or how many mistakes you or I made. Your house needed a daughter-in-law. That was the thing. Your parents have grown old and have survived corona fever with great difficulty. He reminded me of my father and his absence and asked me whether I would want your parents to go away like this? Then he said I was growing, but you were already a grown-up man who was ready for marriage. You were stuck and jobless. At last, he said as soon as I freed you, you would certainly accept the marriage proposals,' she said.

'That's deep,' I replied.

'And you immediately agreed to marry when I liberated you,' she said, her tone filled with anger and pain.

'I didn't have a choice, and you had gone too,' I said.

'And you moved on too quickly,' I said further.

'It was the hardest decision I had ever made in my life. When you left, I realized how lonely I was. My mother also missed you a lot, and she told me many times that she would attend your wedding, but I lacked the courage. It was very difficult to sit up at night and remember the right and wrong and still not be able to call you. This ten-year age difference between us was actually felt by your brother's words. I never even thought about it,' she spoke.

After listening to her words, I deeply dived into grief.

'You grew up. A bit quickly, but you grew up,' I said.

'I didn't have a choice, and this guy—my boyfriend is a very nice guy. My mother knew him and he loves me like I want him to,' she said.

'Did you two have sex?' I asked.

She glanced at me with fierce eyes.

'I felt the same way when you had your wedding night,' she said.

'I missed you a couple of times while making love with my wife,' I said.

'We always miss the void-creators of our life,' she said.

While my eyes were fixed on her, I realized she was also directing her gaze towards me. The similar gaze. We had a great time during the evening, making it a fun and memorable occasion. As the wind blew carelessly, her hair danced and fluttered in the air, creating a mesmerizing wavelike motion. It is possible that her face seemed chubby now, but it could also be because I appeared to be slightly intoxicated. People had gone. Just the two of us. Despite being fully prepared to make that mistake, I knew Rashmi might never forgive me. As I approached her lips at a leisurely pace, she responded by pushing me back.

'Don't do it. I can't be your wife's enemy,' she said.

'You never let me settle. I have been running since I got married. Never able to provide the correct answer to Rashmi. We had stayed in Haridwar and I took her to all the places where we had gone. Just to forget you, and I succeeded, but only for a few days. You had become a pattern. I still couldn't digest the fact that you could leave me and push me to hell. I love my wife very much. Perhaps she saved me from going crazy. But sometimes it feels like maybe I'm still in love with you. Now I don't understand why I can't love both of you. God has made no such provision; rather, society did. Why can't I love Rashmi and Tanu together?' I yelled.

'Ask Rashmi about this question. I'm curious to know the answer,' she chuckled.

'I will definitely seek this question,' I said.

Chapter-24

The Closure

Before leaving, it occurred to me to hug her once, but I could not express that clearly towards her. She and I were standing by her scooty when she abruptly approached and hugged me. This was like I hug my friends. No other feelings were involved. Suddenly, everything changed. It was as if my inner emotions had come to a standstill. We departed. It was getting dark, and I had to leave. This one meeting transformed the tsunami of emotions inside me into a calm pond. Today, I found my peace and corruption inside me seemed to be healed. I dropped her at ISBT, hopped onto my bus, said goodbye to her, and headed towards my home.

'Can't a person love two people at a time?' I asked Rashmi while she was breastfeeding Avni.

'Why would you ask that?' She asked, worried.

'In ancient time, polygamy was common. Why in today's world it is banned?' I asked.

'Do you consider polygamy a good thing? Was our Lord Shiva or Lord Ram polygamous?' She asked.

'What about lord Krishna? Many theories say...'

'False theories. He married only Rukmini. He rescued other women from the giant and, in order to pay their respect, all of them considered him as their deity, like Meera,' she interrupted me.

'Our Ancient kings.'

'To enhance their kingdom. To make allies with other kings. Not out of love,' she said.

'So, a person can't love multiple people,' I said.

'Actually, we can love multiple people, but it's not wise to live with all of them. The fewer people we share our bond with, the less complicated our life will be. The Karma theory believes in detachments, not attachments. Attachments bring weakness to a person, and as a human being, we are not here just to survive, we are here to achieve great things and this could only be done if our body and mind would remain integrated,' she said.

'I know all of this. I know even further. But it's my heart that is searching for an answer that could satisfy him, as it wants Tanu back in either way.' I thought.

'What are you reading nowadays?' Rashmi asked.

'Why would you ask?'

'You know everything about relationships and how they work, still you ask foolish questions,' she said.

'I know I'm wrong and I'm asking something that I couldn't even suggest to anyone, but the heart wants what

the heart wants. I want my wrong to become the right,' I thought.

'Out of curiosity, nothing else,' I said.

'Do you still miss your ex?' I asked her.

'Sometimes, not in a glorious way. A faded memory,' she said.

'We frequently miss the void-creators of our lives,' I said.

'Some people come into our lives for a brief period, like visitors. When they come, it feels like permanent, yet destiny separates us anyhow and we keep thinking, cursing and blaming, but nothing happens. This is our cycle of karma. We are bound to come here to lighten the burden of karma. Our karmas are stuck with them, and theirs with us. Lord Ram tells something to Laxman about karma and destiny before going into exile,' she said.

'Tell me.'

'After being exiled, Lakshman tells Shri Ram that this is wrong according to our beliefs, and we must oppose our father. Then Shri Ram tells him that look, I was going to become the king and now I have nothing left, and I am going into the exile. There can be no argument about the way everything has happened because I have done no work that would cause pain to Mother Kaikai. I have always treated her like Mother Kaushalya, and she also did not discriminate between me and Bharat. So, it is illogical for her to have a notion that would make me unhappy. This signifies that my destiny wants to lead me down a different road and, until I follow that path, I will not realize my karma and true purpose. Therefore, brother, it is absolutely appropriate to go into exile at this very moment. That is why we should trust in the creator's plan,' she said.

Hearing this, I realized that even after Tanu left, my life had improved even more. A wonderful wife, a sweet daughter, and we were all on the right track, but I am still holding onto something that is ruining my life. It would have been better if I had let things go.

'I met my ex today. I wondered what my brother told her the day she left me,' I said.

For the next one hour, I briefed Rashmi about my relationship with Tanu and her family and whatever I talked to Tanu. She was astonished, but not upset.

'When I agreed to marry you, I knew that no matter what happened, I would never look back. Destiny picked this course for me, and I accepted it wholeheartedly. People come to mind because it is beyond our control whether or not we remember them. What is within our control is what we must do. Keep hurting yourself by clinging to the memories, or simply accept the reality. When Lord Shri Ram can move forward, keeping the decision of supreme destiny without complaining to anyone, what maze are you trapped in? And Tanu had also moved forward the same day when your brother revealed the reality to her. She accepted it, keeping the pain aside,' she elaborated.

'I deserved a proper closure. It's not like I'm still chasing her, but I couldn't bury her. Every time I think I did it, something happens, and she reappears in front of me,' he said.

'You had your proper closure, but you don't want to understand it. Either it's in your male ego that a nineteen-year-old girl could leave you or you have become too blind to see,' she said in a louder voice.

'Which solution are you looking for right now? I presume she has given you appropriate closure, or you want to go on further trips with her. Ask her if she wants to meet you,' she said.

'Do not talk to me like that. I am looking for help from you.'

'You deserve that tone.'

'I think both of you should meet,' I suggested.

'Why should I meet her? Is there any kind of deal that you're going to make with her?' She asked.

'That would make everything normal for me. I don't want her mother to remember me as a devil. She had always been kind to me.'

'And that would make everything worse for us if you keep insisting and her mother would think that, anyway. Breaking her daughter's heart would make any mother think of a guy as a devil, and you financially deceived them, too.'

'She didn't know about me and Tanu.'

'Mothers have a way of knowing who their daughters have feelings for. By now, she would have realized it from her daughter's tears, and you're already seen as a villain in her family. You had your doubts, and you cleared them with her; now what? I should be angry with you for what you've done behind my back,' she said further.

'You're hurting me and I did nothing out of the limits. She is not a stupid girl.'

'Then why are you still chasing her? What if my ex just popped into my life to know about my wellbeing and whereabouts? How would you feel?'

'You had your closure with him. You still wanted to talk to that dirty-minded person who was asking for a non-tilting bed from your mother?'

'That doesn't make him an overall horrible person.'

'So, you're taking sides now?'

'I am not. Just as you feel uneasy when I discuss my ex, I feel the same way too, and you're constantly putting that topic on the table. Even you have met with her. No wife would tolerate her husband meeting with his ex, no matter how formally they are meeting.'

'I know I have become a mess, but I'm just trying to be as strong as you. I wanted to eliminate these shitty emotions, just not the person,' I said, holding her in my arms.

'People bring the emotions back. We are not robots.'

'That is what I am trying to communicate. I wanted her to be as normal in my life as the rest of the world. I don't want to have any fantasies for her. You got your closure, and I want mine. I want to make amends and make things right.'

'Then go, do as you please. Just don't irritate me.'

'It's fine. Don't meet her. I won't meet her ever again. Chapter closed. I have nothing left to do with her,' I said.

The conversation did not end well. Rashmi stopped talking to me. We became strangers for a couple of days. Nothing more than formalities took place. My parents were observing. I didn't have the words to make her understand. A week later, she told me she wanted to go home.

'Is it for a particular reason?' I asked.

'No, I feel suffocated. I just want to spend some time with my mom,' she replied.

She intentionally avoided looking me in the eye.

'Why are you making this a difficult situation? I only want to transform a person who my heart and thoughts have transformed someone extraordinary into a regular one,' I said.

'Did she tell you she wants to meet me?'

'Before dating her, I wanted things back to normal. She said nothing. She is content with her life,' I said.

'Why do you have such a strong desire for her to meet me? If you want to meet her or her family, simply go. Why are you including me? Why do you continue to give me the impression that you are desperately chasing her? Is it you also desire a certificate from her to confirm that you have moved on?' She spoke louder and harsher.

'I think that might be the proper closure. Accepting realities, forgiving each other and being glad to see each other's happy,' I said gracefully.

'If you care about their family, they are always welcome at my home,' she finally remarked serenely.

'I have long waited to hear this,' I remarked with excitement.

'Please don't go home; we'll go together next week,' I begged. After a half-hour of head marching, she eventually agreed.

I texted Tanu:

'Listen, why don't you come to my home? With your mother and brother. Pay a visit to my daughter. I am inviting you.'

'You're inviting me to your home? Your brother won't like it,' she replied.

'He won't mind,' I wrote.

'I recently broke up with him. Going home is not possible for me. I have to learn to live alone,' she said.

'What!! How could this happen? I saw the love in his eyes for you. He could die for you,' I texted back.

'That's the problem. He had become overly possessive. He didn't let me breathe,' she wrote.

'So, what now?' I asked.

'I need some time. The problem began following the day we met. He became angry with me because I was drunk. Constantly asking who I was drinking with. He couldn't believe that I could drink one beer on my own,' she responded.

'A man always feels animosity even towards the wind that touches his beloved,' I said.

'Guys are crazy. Trying to own girls.'

'Some are.'

'This is the perfect time. Visiting my home would be like breathing in free air.'

'You have a beautiful wife and daughter. Still, you want me to come there?'

'I want everything to be normal around me.'

'Had it ever happened? Normal things happen to normal people and you can't be a normal person. You can pretend to be.'

'Teasing?'

'No, that's who you are. You have a habit of clinging to things, and I'm sure you have already disrupted your wife's peace.'

'That was why I invited you and your family. So, she could feel everything was fine.'

'You told her everything?'

'What everything? I can't recall everything. Just the key ones: the link with your family and our connection, our interactions, and a few conversations.'

'Is she okay? After hearing what you said.'

'She thinks I am being absurd. She might be a little jealous of you.'

'We should not have met. It was a mistake on my part to respond to you. I always thought of you as a mature man, yet you once again disappointed me. I am an unmarried girl. Even if I had a breakup, I still believe that one day I would find the right one, but you are only hurting your wife. She is clearly a good woman who has not hit you yet. However, if she has mentally separated herself from you, you can never reclaim her heart. So, you nerdy, go to your wife and do what she says, and when I have to come to your home, I will tell you myself. Bye,' she said.

'What am I to do with these women?' I asked myself.

I just lay in bed, and my daughter gazed at me. That little angel kept looking at me, and after a minute, she began crying. She did not lift her hands to enter my arms or greet me with a smile, as she always did. She just cried out. Something was clearly wrong with me. I tried to pick her up, but she cried even harder. She did not want to come to me. Even my daughter was rejecting me. Something horrible was inside me, and it was obvious on my face. Rashmi approached and grabbed her. She stopped crying, stared at me for a few seconds, and then ignored me. She might be looking for her daddy in me, and I had transformed into someone else.

I entered another room, closed my eyes, and lay down on the sofa. I attempted to disengage myself from everything. Random thoughts were swirling around in my head. I needed to work on myself urgently.

Throughout the week that followed, I consistently had a headache. I felt depressed every single day, without exception. I felt my life was purposeless. Rashmi was simply fulfilling her responsibilities towards me and our household. My parents were watching me behave oddly. I slept by myself during the night. I was constantly seeking closure. I could not determine exactly what I wanted. I asked a few questions to myself that day.

'Do I want two women in my life? Rashmi as my wife and Tanu as my girlfriend? Seriously?'

'Do I want Tanu in my life just to fulfil my sexual desires?'

'Do I desire to make Tanu experience the same pain as she inflicted on me?'

'Why do I feel such an intense desire to reconcile with both her and her mother? Why couldn't I leave them hating me for the rest of my life? I have done it for many people.'

Then I remembered the book *The Power of Your Subconscious Mind* by Joseph Murphy. I allowed my subconscious to come to the conclusion. I was observing the Ghats of Haridwar, the red scooty's odometer, Tanu's hair, Rashmi playing with Avni, my father scratching his grown-out white beard, and my brother having beer and possibly making love with someone.

It was the first time I tried to avoid overthinking a particular topic or individual. I did this for the second day, too. The third day, I came to a conclusion. I realized I had no intention of hurting Tanu in any way and I couldn't stand deceiving my wife either. This conclusion prompted me to consider an alternative perspective.

The principle of gravity applies to every object that has mass. It makes no difference whether or not the object knows about it. A person who understands gravity will fall to the ground if dropped in the air, as will a stone, a non-living object that is unaware of gravity.

Fate, much like gravity, impacts us all, but our karmas determine how it shapes our lives, converting it into destiny. The fate of a falling stone, whether it reaches the ground or breaks along the way, is determined by the manner in which it falls, highlighting the critical role of its falling process.

If you hold a belief in karma, you find that destiny guides you through various challenging situations throughout your entire lifetime; however, if you maintain your integrity, you will ultimately make the choices that are right instead of simply taking the easy way out. Decisions with a vision. You have to fall, but you don't have to free fall. Free fall is a fate, but when we cause a resistance to avoid free fall, it becomes the flow of destiny and it is caused by our decisions.

There are individuals who are inherently tough with powerful characters, and they demonstrate their resilience by accepting their destiny and making the right decisions, not the easy ones, much like Lord Ram did, which ultimately led to their greatness.

The women, both Tanu and Rashmi, had a significant impact on me by teaching me a valuable lesson. In my opinion, both of these women possess high values and morals, and I would consider them to be of great worth. There were distinct reasons for Tanu to leave me and for Rashmi to accept me, each driven by their own unique circumstances. For Tanu, leaving me was necessary in order to experience growth, whereas Rashmi had to choose me for the sake of stability. Tanu unintentionally followed Lord Rama's story of exile, whereas Rashmi had it engraved in her head. Tanu had a vision when she left me. I eventually realized that Tanu might easily forgive me for my mistake, but she wanted to go on, and my brother fuelled that vision in her. She was a nineteen-year-old girl who made the daring decision not to accept me back into her life. Rashmi did the same thing with her ex. They had a five-year relationship, but she left him because of her long-term vision for me!!

The night I requested my wife to sleep beside me while Avni slept on the other side. She did. She remained hopeful that her partner had not yet become entirely polluted. Her head rested on my forearm.

'Lord Ram took a wise decision to go into exile. Like he embraced his destiny and made the right choice. I am accepting it too. Most of my life, I have often done what I thought was right. Achieving the closure I needed, I have let go of my stubbornness about doing everything appropriately. The most appropriate thing happened to me on the day I married you. Forgive me for the pain I've caused you,' I said.

'Finally, you deceived the devil. For a moment I thought you had gone,' she said.

'Nah, I haven't deceived the devil. I was the devil,' I said.

'What about making amends and doing things right?'

'Deep down, I believe her mother will eventually see that I am not that wrong. She is a kind lady.'

She rested in my arms, and we fell asleep while talking. When I awoke in the morning, it felt like another Corona-like fever had passed. My heart was light. After an excellent breakfast, I resumed work. Gradually, I realized that if you hold a light stone in your hand for an extended period, it will grow so heavy that it would inflict suffering to your hand.

The calmness I've been seeking has finally arrived in my heart. I came to the realization that whenever I felt something itchy inside me, it was because of the way I was acting. My perspective and perception of the world. Tanu and Rashmi are not the ones. I kept going to the work for months with no glitch to my heart and one day when I returned home from work, a steel-grey car was parked in front of my house. I recognized the vehicle the moment I saw it. I smiled slightly as I gazed at the car. The Lord Shiva idol was still on the dashboard. There were some scratches, too. When I stepped inside, I noticed my daughter was playing comfortably in Tanu's lap, while her mother was engaged in conversation with Rashmi and my mother.

The teacups were empty, showing that I had arrived late. Everyone seemed happy. I sat next to her mother and sought about her well-being. She mentioned nothing outdated or clichéd. She was really honest with me. A stunning costume was kept on Avni's bed.

Evening was approaching, and it was time for them to return. Rashmi and I came to drop them off outside. Tanu, as usual, abruptly released the car's clutch, and the car jerked forward. I burst into laughter. She understood why I was laughing.

'She won't improvise,' I said to her mother.

Her mother laughed too.

Come to think of it, what was it that was holding me back for so long?

All I can say is that it is good for those who have received closure, and those who have not should follow the creator's plan, such as Lord Shri Ram did. Instead of relying on fate, we should take control of our lives and shape our own destiny. His teachings show us that going into exile might reveal the realistic goal of one's life rather than being a king.

Jai Shri Ram

www.ingramcontent.com/pod-product-compliance
Lightning Source LLC
LaVergne TN
LVHW061608070526
838199LV00078B/7209